HONEY &

SULPHUR

CB555-10: Honey & Sulphur
ISBN: 978-0-9962768-5-6

Carrion Blue 555
Chicopee MA / Lambertville NJ
carrionblue555@gmail.com

Cover art copyright ©2019 by Matthew Revert.
www.matthewrevert.com
Carrion Blue 555 logo designed by Brent Carpentier.

All work copyright ©2019 by the respective author.

All rights reserved. No part of this book may be reproduced or transmitted in any form or by any means, electronic or mechanical, including photocopying, recording, or by any information storage and retrieval system, without the written consent of the publisher, except where permitted by law.

All persons in this book are fictitious, and any resemblance that may seem to exist to actual persons living or dead is purely coincidental or for purposes of satire or parody. All content is original to the author or included under fair use. All copyrights and trademarks are reserved by their respectful owners. This is a work of fiction.

"This is Heaven alright, but there's a man outside with a gun."
—Cardiacs, "What Paradise is Like"

TABLE OF CONTENTS

I: WITH ROOT ABOVE AND BRANCH BELOW

Froth of the Liquid Jade
    Kyle E. Miller 9

A Cambrian Vengeance
    Ian Ableson 31

River Vessel
    LaVa Payne 37

II: TERATOMA PANORAMA

For the Hidden Woman
    Virginia Chase Sutton 41

New World Fruit
    Tiffany Morris 43

Boschiary
    Frederick L. Shiels 47

A Paint of View
    Dr. Jackie Ferris 49

Sentient Palate
    Sara Tantlinger   73

Within the garden, running
    R. Bremner   75

Paradisium Voluptatis
    Joanna Koch   77

III: THE LAST LAST CHANCE PARADE

Why Do Birds Suddenly Appear?
    Rajiv Moté   99

The Gall
    M. Regan   111

Gatekeeper
    Andrea L. Staum   127

The Garden of Metamorphosis
    Terje Nordin   129

This volume lacks an introduction, for, like the forbidden garden, it is best to stumble headlong into its dazzling and loathsome grandeur, with no guiding hand, with no attending voice.

NOWEDTA

ANDINGIN

SURETHIN

OTHINGBU

RFLIESAN

EARTSOFME

OGSFALL

ERLINGE

WITH ROOT ABOVE

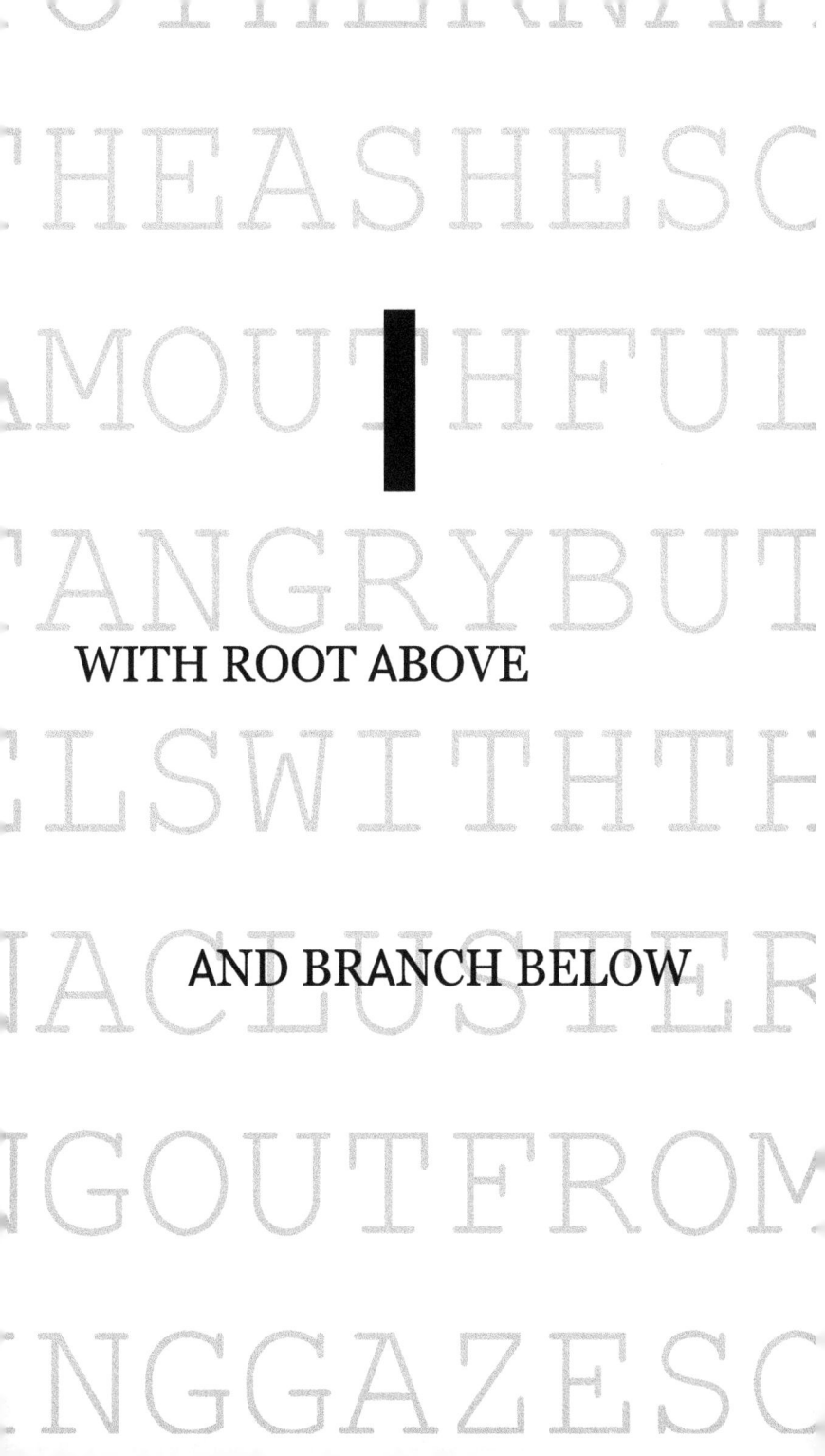

AND BRANCH BELOW

FROTH OF THE LIQUID JADE
Kyle E. Miller

Frograin fell on the cousins' back porch tea party. The pink porcelain kettle rattled with the weight of a fallen bullfrog, and tiny tree frogs splashed into the cups, freckling the tablecloth with drops of green tea. They came down singing and didn't stop, all colors and all sizes, some big and spotted like leopards and others tiny, translucent, as fragile as glass. Sunlight made rainbows in the webbing between their toes.

"I can't see what the problem is," Vervain said, smiling.

"Oh no," Cousin Cattooth said. "None of your imaginary problems talk. I didn't call you down here only to have you give us your pretty lecture and leave us in the lurch."

"You remember that, huh?"

For every ogreling who preyed on the virgin boys of a highland village, there were two badgers in a cellar. Or faulty wiring and flickering lamps. Or juicy grapes of gossip bursting even before they fell from the vine. Never underestimate the imagination of people with nothing to worry about, Vervain liked to say: they always find something.

"Oh, I remember." Cousin Cattooth stood, bumping the table with his paunch and upsetting the teacups once again. His tunic was too narrow and too short, and thick red belly hair curled upward and out. "I can see this problem, cousin. See it, hear it, feel it," he plucked the frog from his cup and held it to his nose, "and smell it."

Vervain could too: the stagnant green murk of a sunbaked pond. "You're not going to hurt him, are you?" He nodded toward the frog in his cousin's hand.

Cousin Cattooth tossed the frog into the flowerbed, fetched an umbrella from underneath the porch steps, and stuck it in the center of the table. He pushed the lever and the umbrella chuckled open. Frog shadows fell on the purple canvas with a splat and slipped off. One clung to the edge, meaty thighs pumping the air.

"I would feed them all to the cat if I could." Cousin Cattooth sat down again and sipped his frog flavored tea. "But then you'd be a sniveling ball of snot and useless to us. I'll pay you well."

"You know I don't take payment, cousin. And doubly for you. You're my only family." Cattooth had always been there for him, and Vervain planned to return the favor as often and as best as he could. "Just tell me what happened."

"We'll talk payment later. Anyway." Cousin Cattooth took a sip of tea. "Did you ever catch raindrops in your mouth?"

"Sure. As a kid." Vervain had to speak up now to be heard over the frogs. Village sounds blended with the frogs' voices: the scouring of saucepans, the wail of an infant, the dumping of water out a window.

"And kids still do. And I don't blame them, but they thought it would be funny to catch frogs in their mouths, and for a while it was. A few of us even tried, though not me of course." He paused. "Cousin, some of these frogs are poisonous. Toxic."

"Oh."

"Now you see the problem. The boy turned as purple as this sunshade." Cousin Cattooth sighed and itched his neck. There were scratches there, pink and ready to bleed. "A giant frog has moved in near the pond, cousin, and it's bringing this rain down on us as punishment. The rain comes and goes as it pleases, starting, stopping freely. I don't know why and I don't know how and I'm sure I don't even want to know. Get rid of the frog, cousin. And get rid of the frograin."

"How big of a frog?"

"I saw it from afar and came no closer. Its tongue could take out a man, a whip rivaled in size and persuasive power only by my wife's, I assure you."

Vervain chuckled and sipped his tea. He had long ago learned how to humor his cousin. A frog's head appeared in the froth on the surface of his tea, peeking out as if through the scum of a pond. Vervain lifted him out and onto the table.

"I don't know, but you will. This is your life's work. Hobnobs and goosels and shesep-ankhs. You're a madman, bless you. They are your family. Besides me, of course. Anyway, cousin, this is your day." He held his teacup high for a toast.

Vervain clinked his cup to his cousin's and took a sip. His cousin was right: he was always falling in love with the monsters he was meant to dispose of, not romantically (though that had happened once or twice as well), but in the way of companions and brethren. What others found awful and ugly, he found charming and fair. Because he was ugly, orphaned, and estranged, he counted himself among them. They were the problems he was meant to solve by untangling the knot of human-to-nonhuman communication, with negotiation or healing or else with the painless prick of a lethal injection. He had only used that once in seven years of practice, and he was proud of that, proud always to have found another way.

"I would offer you a room," Cousin Cattooth said, "but we're rebuilding the house. The bathroom is in the kitchen, you know? It's a mess. But you'll have a room at the Ingress of the Egret. It's paid for. Ah-ah! It's the least we can do for our hero."

Praise flustered Vervain, and he stammered and then trailed off, sniffing the air.

"Cousin?"

Vervain smelled the ego before he saw it, a foul combination of vinegar and cloves. He turned and spotted a rangy stranger in the distance. He was holding a black parasol to deflect the falling frogs, and his ego was wrapped around his neck like a pink and fleshy scarf.

"What's he doing here?" Vervain asked. He was ashamed to feel so much disgust, and so suddenly, but there it was.

Cousin Cattooth's eyes wandered. "Ah, well. I was going to tell you."

"Tell me what?"

"Do you know him?"

"No. But I know his type."

"He won't interfere. I promise. Carnelian's his name. He only wants what's left. After you're done, I mean. Some kind of gemstone inside the frog, big because this one's big, and valuable. He's a budding merchant, I guess, and—"

"Cousin. What are you talking about?"

"Uh, well, if you don't succeed. If you can't make the frograin stop, he's, uh. He's going to kill the frog and cut the stone from its head."

The frograin stopped.

Vervain massaged his temples. He had a sudden headache.

***

The Village in the Damps was arranged in three lobes like the leaf of one of the sassafras trees that forested the area. There were simple stone houses, a few gnarled gazebos, and a watchtower for each of the three lobes, situated on the edge of the village where the forest ended and the fields began, where sleepless sentries stood, spyglasses in hand.

Lilac bushes draped clumps of purple flowers

over every roof and door. The warmth and humidity made the blossoms smell a little boggy and overripe, but Vervain paused to smell them anyway. He was headed toward the point where the three lobes joined, the heart of the village where the oldest trees grew. Farther on was the pond, the soggy meadow, and the expanse of wetlands beyond. All that dampness crept into the village, mostly sheltered from the sun by the canopy of sassafras leaves, and Vervain heard villagers exchanging complaints of sore throats, stuffy noses, and aching bones. The farmers and gardeners were in their fields and gardens, picking frogs from yesterday's furrows. Cats lazed in a patch of sunlight, and the villagers hustled and bustled to and fro. Somewhere, someone's radio played "The March of the Blue Heron."

Though he was there to help, Vervain drew overlong looks and suspicious glances. Ever since he had set foot in the village, he felt a profound restlessness, and it was not his own. All the villagers, including his cousin, seemed somehow troubled and restive. He would have to look into that later, after he had found the frog.

On the trail to the pond, flower petals covered the path as thick and sweet as buttered cake. Petals gave way to soil, rich and brown, and then watercress, ivy, and saxifrage. Mayapples covered the forest floor like fairy umbrellas, and giant horsetail presaged the pond ahead. Vervain picked a stalk of horsetail, tucked one end into the other, and hung it around his neck.

He smelled the pond before he saw it, dank and decomposing, and he heard it too: frogs croaking, fish leaping, and, as he came over the mounded bank, the diving splash of turtles alarmed by his approach. And there it was, a still green pool covered in scum and yellow lilies.

There was power here.

Vervain removed his boots. He would head

down to the edge of the pond and wait for the frog to appear. After all, he was trespassing, and the frog would no doubt try to defend his territory. But on his first step toward the water, Vervain lost his footing in the soft mossy ground and fell. He slid down the embankment, knocking his head on a log, sending spotted red salamanders back into their burrows.

When he sat up, he was staring into the eye of a frog. The pool of black in the center was as big as the palm of his hand, and the ring of gold green around it was full of swimming shapes. Flecks of green, spots of gold, darting around like tadpoles underwater, and Vervain saw a meadow, green and full. He saw rain, real rain, wet and gray, and then a puddle, a pool, a swamp soaking through. He watched rabbit warrens flood and two fox kits drown. He watched grass wither and blacken, and he saw the first blooms of algae, the arrival of snails, the birth of lilies, the accumulation of scum, the coming of waterfowl and snakes and frogs, and he saw a pond.

This pond.

The pond he was once again staring at, avoiding the frog's magic gaze.

"What was that?" he said, still watching the water. The shallows teemed with wriggling black tadpoles. Bluegill, perch, and ingret—a small freshwater fish with violet scales—darted away.

"A little history," the frog said. His voice came from the depths of his swollen throat, as full of tension as a guitar string.

When Vervain had the courage to look again, he saw just how large the frog was. He could swallow a man whole, just as his cousin had said. He resembled a bullfrog more than any other species, although on his skin Vervain saw more shades of green than he knew existed. The frog was teaching him colors.

And the frog's leg was mangled by a rusty toothed trap, too small even to catch a bear, but large enough to maim, to cripple. Looking at it, Vervain felt a pang in his own leg.

"What's your name, or what should I call you?" He always began with a patient's name, and while he answered, he would circle around and inspect the wound.

But the frog stretched out his right front leg, tripped him, and pinned him to the ground. Vervain could feel the wet earth sucking at his body, as if tasting him before the sudden fatal gulp.

"I'm here to help."

The frog leaned down and sniffed, his nostrils flaring. "The trap was set in the old fane across the way where I now slumber, the sanctum being abandoned. But you have never set foot there."

Still pinned, Vervain twisted his neck and looked at the other side of the pond, at stone ruins he hadn't noticed before, overgrown and cavernous. He could just barely make out the head of a statue poking through white anemones.

"No, I haven't. Poachers did this. They want some silly stone inside your head. Please. Let me up, and I'll get the trap off faster than it got on."

The frog relented, and Vervain stood, snatched his pharmacopeia bag from the weeds, and bent down to examine the wound. "Now, will you tell me your name?"

"Can you sing? My name is a song, but Dwyn will do until the end."

"Dwyn. You're going to be fine." Vervain went to work on the trap, trying to be gentle. "Idiots. They never meant to kill you, only stop you from moving so fast. Hold still if you can." He liked to talk to his patients. Words were a potent distraction. "There's more than one party after you. Or the stone in your head, rather. Ah! There we go." He threw the trap aside and reached for his bag.

"A stone inside my head?"

"The frogstone. It's a human myth. Well. I suppose it could be real, a calcium deposit. Or some other mineral, too small to detect in normal frogs, but, according to their logic, large enough to be worth something if it came from a frog your size. But I doubt it."

"So they call it a frogstone."

"What?" Vervain risked a look at Dwyn's eye. "It's real?"

"If they want it, you better take it."

"I don't want it," Vervain said, returning to his work. "You won't even need stiches. Now a healing salve. And this one will keep the flies away."

"Keep the flies away?" Dwyn asked. "Why would I want to do that?"

Vervain paused, pale cream dripping from his fingers. "So you don't get flystrike, but wait. Aren't flies a little small for you?"

"Like plankton for a whale," Dwyn said.

Vervain laughed and patted the frog on the thigh. He was no longer afraid, no longer worried that he might offend the regal frog.

When he was finished disinfecting and wrapping the wound, Vervain sat down on the bank beside Dwyn. He was sweating, and the mosquitos were beginning to bite. The humidity was worse than the day before. The air was as thick as water. Flies became fish. Birds became sharks. At night, owls soared overhead like silent manta rays.

"You'll walk tomorrow, the day after at the latest." Vervain yawned and stretched himself out on the bank. "This place is enchanted. You must know. There's something here." He could feel the magic, deeply rooted, planted in the pond like an old anchor, festooned with fairy snails and algae. Or maybe it was Dwyn himself, and he was already losing himself in the seductive tangle of the frog's mammoth will.

Maybe he wanted to be lost.

"The pond is not what it once was," Dwyn was saying. "The fane was once occupied by a loyal cleric, and the pond was a place of peace. I remember. I remember warm emerald evenings you thought might never end, and the flies bulged with juices, and the toads left well enough alone."

How old he must be, Vervain thought, how wise. And yet he felt something black and rotten in him too. The reservoir of dark water in which all things could see their reflection. He thought of Carnelian then, and his own fear of becoming not a monster, but a man, flawed and full of turmoil.

Dwyn's voice shook Vervain from his thoughts. "And the pond is not now what it will be. And soon."

A shiver crept down Vervain's neck, and black-billed ducks took flight. He wondered if he should let himself slip farther into the frog's feelings, or if he was better off not becoming involved.

"You should take the stone now," Dwyn said.

"But I don't want it."

"All the more reason it should be yours."

"But everyone will still think you have it, don't you see? They'll still hunt you down. They'll still try to kill you and kick open your jaw like the lid of a treasure chest. You have to leave."

"They will come anyway, but they won't get it because I won't have it."

"You have to leave!"

"They mustn't get ahold of it. And they won't. You'll see. Now, open up."

"Open wha—"

Vervain had never been skilled at remaining neutral, at keeping his distance. He always had to steal another glance into the cloudy well of monstrous thoughts and emotions.

Vervain didn't see the tongue, it went so fast, but he felt it. Like a kiss.

And something fell into the old pond in his

heart—the sound of water.
Plop!

***

The egret who nested in the dusty rafters of the inn preened herself as Vervain sat down in the common room with the boy who had found him by the pond. An ivory feather drifted down and the boy caught it before it hit the mud scuffed floor.

"Food? Wine? Something to smoke?" the innkeeper asked. She was a lumbering ancient with a single tooth and a nimbus of ghostly hair around her head.

"Just water, please," Vervain said.

"Holier than all that, eh?"

"No, I'm just not hungry." Vervain was always having to explain himself to those who couldn't understand his contentment.

The innkeeper shrugged and lumbered away.

"What about me?" the boy asked.

"I'm not sure she saw you. I'm not even sure she saw me. She seems halfway between life and death." Another restless soul, he thought. "You can share my water. So I was unconscious when you found me?"

"Out cold, doctor."

"Call me Vervain. And no sign of the frog?"

"Nothin'."

"Then he must have gone back to... ah, I better not say."

"You can trust me. I like frogs. I saved one from the dog when it rained. But there's not gonna be more frograin, is there?" Disappointment colored his voice.

"There's better magic down at the pond," Vervain said. The innkeeper returned with a tankard of water, and Vervain took a drink. It felt a little scratchy going down, as if he was about to catch a cold. "What's your name, anyway?"

"Dewlark, the butcher's son."

"Ah. And you'll be taking over the family trade? You're about that age."

"I don't want to. But da says I must, and ma too. I don't like it. I don't like the blood, and the eyes, the way they look when they're dead, like an empty glass."

Vervain winced. There was still something off about the whole village. A thorn in its paw. A restless ghost in the air. And yet he had felt immense power down at the pond. Magic, ancient and dank, ready to be poured into receptive vessels. Maybe he would stay a few more days and see if he could lay at least one burden to rest.

"I want to be a baker," Dewlark went on, "but da says it's not a man's trade. Da says I have to be a man."

Vervain removed the horsetail from around his neck and leaned over the table to hook it around Dewlark's head. "If you let it, this will ward off leeches, mosquitos, and other swamp pests, so maybe someday you can run away, through the wetlands and into the fairy wood. They need bakers there, to make enough sweets to please the king and queen."

Dewlark's eyes lit up, and then the door squeaked open, and Vervain cursed under his breath.

Carnelian stood in the door.

"Word is, you're all finished, and the frograin will never come again." He stepped up to the table and gave Dewlark a shove. "It's time for grown up talk. Go play in the dirt."

"Hey! I was sitting here first!"

"If you don't get out, I'll give you toadskin," Carnelian said. Brown wrinkles and warts flickered in and out on Dewlark's arms, and he ran out of the inn, tripping and scraping his knee on the doorstep.

"That was too much," Vervain said.

"Eh, he'll forget about it tomorrow." Carnelian

sat at the table, and his ego slid off his shoulders and pooled in his lap. It peeked its head above the rim of the table and watched Vervain with pale, indolent eyes. It had no lips, only a curve of wrinkled gums and a single crooked fang. "Well? Did you drive the frog off, then?"

"I healed him, and now he can hop out of here, which is looking increasingly appealing."

"Ah, right. You healed him. With your empathy magic."

"You know that's not how it works. I wouldn't waste my energy trying to change the world to my liking or anyone else's."

"Oh, but I would. Because I'm an evil sorcerer. I get it. You're not very good at this, are you?" Carnelian looked around impatiently. "Where's that lich of an innkeeper?" He pounded the table with one fist.

Carnelian was a dangerous man for Vervain to be around, like any who could distill their wills into flesh and bone. He would have to keep constant guard, lest he be drawn into the labyrinth of Carnelian's self. He would wander there for a long time, slowly losing his own personality, trying to hold onto it and thus losing it all the more, taking on more and more of Carnelian's traits. It was a malicious game of mirrors, and Vervain wasn't sure he could win.

Carnelian spat on the floor, and his ego tried to mimic him, though it had no saliva of its own. "I'm not staying longer than I have to. This place is intolerable."

"I quite like it."

"It's humid. Saps the energy from your bones. There's something ill here. Probably that frog, still haunting the pond. And if it is, it's my turn to try and get rid of it. It's a danger."

"It's a treasure."

"No. The treasure is inside. Apothecaries grind it down and bottle it and idiots buy it believing it will trick their cocks into thinking they still find their wives attractive."

"You know, there's a better world somewhere on the other side of yourself."

Carnelian barked a chuckle, and his ego smiled, if such a thing was possible. "I used to be like you. Did you know that? Wrapped up in other people's feelings. So careful and cautious, watching my step. Afraid to look inside and see that I was not a holy man." He laughed. "If you're the tadpole, I'm the frog."

"Fuck off, Carnelian."

Carnelian's ego lashed out and sunk its single fang into Vervain's wrist with an almost imperceptible poke that quickly rose to a wild burning.

Vervain didn't move his body, but his mind was busy searching, questing up and around for something useful. Not the heron above, nor her feathers, not the tankard on the table, nor the water within—only the cool clear magic of quenched thirst—but there was a little magic down below: a few grains of sand fallen in a crack in the floorboards, blue sand from a faraway beach brought there on the soles of some vagabond's boots. And before they were grains of sand, they were part of a tiny snake-shaped bottle that fit in the palm of your hand, and that bottle stoppered a poison so potent it could kill a dozen men with a drop. Vervain found the magic in the world and let it change him.

The ego released his wrist, and its venom bubbled out of the red dot of his wound.

Carnelian snorted and let his ego slide up his arm to settle on his shoulders. "Cute trick."

Vervain was still recovering and couldn't speak. He could feel the venom bubbling in his bloodstream, like ants somehow let inside.

"You're never going to be the same again," Carnelian said, and he was right: already, Vervain could feel the hardening of his constitution. And he knew that although he would be immune to poisons and venoms of all kinds, so would his body be slow to benefit from medicine.

"All these years of your little tricks." Carnelian stood. "How do you manage to hold on to yourself?"

Vervain managed to gasp a couple of words before Carnelian turned and left: "I don't."

***

Vervain was awakened the next morning by frogs dripping through the ceiling and onto his eyes. The roof was leaking. The heat and humidity glued him to his bed. The windows were fogged, and the floor sweated with condensation. The world was melting away.

And worse still, the frograin had returned, and Carnelian would be hunting for Dwyn.

Vervain lurched out of bed, but his legs would not hold his weight. His body ached, and his throat was full of knots. It was as if he had swallowed a candy lozenge and it had gotten stuck going down.

He reached up to massage his throat and quickly pulled his hand back at what he felt there. A wave of hot panic rose through his body. It took all his energy to reach the mirror in his room's tiny tiled bathroom, and, pulling himself up onto the edge of the sink, he saw that his throat had swollen overnight to the size of an orange.

He had heard that the process of creating an ego was painful, a swift and private splitting of the self. Several days of anguish for a lifetime of companionship and loyal assistance. He began to sweat. His tongue ached. Was this the forming of his ego? Had he become too wrapped up in Carnelian's feelings the day before, or had his fears been right all along?

Would he wake tomorrow and find his ego sleeping beside him?

Somehow, he returned to his bed, thinking of the darkness in his heart.

He was insensible for seven days. On the second, he had visions of lily pads and the cleric who rose from beneath them with a golden lily scepter that called rain. On the third, he dreamed of a world without frogs, some past or future or parallel world on which the sea was boiling and there was born a child who would never see a frog, and that child was him. He woke in tears. On the fourth, he hungered and craved the mosquitos that came in through the broken casement window. On the fifth and sixth he vomited in agony and watched figures pass in and out of his room. They spoke to him, but he could not respond. And on the seventh, he felt all the creatures in the village, every part of the knotted, tangled food chain: spider-eating frogs and frog-eating water spiders, snakes of increasing lengths and girths, and, at night, horned and taloned owls to pick off the midnight peepers.

On the eighth, he was shaken awake.

"Vervain! Vervain!"

He smiled. "You're wearing the necklace."

It was Dewlark and he had tear marks down his cheeks. "They're going to kill him! They found him!"

"What? Who did? Found who?"

"The frog! Carnelian!"

"Show me," Vervain said.

Dewlark pulled a wooden wheelchair beside the bed and helped Vervain into it. He had come prepared. He must have known, must have visited during the past seven days, and that would explain the meals placed next to Vervain's bed: a cup of tea, eggs scrambled with swamp spices, roasted potatoes, and biscuits. He had eaten everything but the eggs, which seemed suddenly nauseating and somehow offensive.

The stairs were difficult, but Cousin Cattooth arrived to help, and they made it into the common room and out the door. Dewlark pushed and pulled, struggling when the wheels got tangled in moss and toadstools or when the whole thing started to sink into the ground. All along the trail, Vervain shouted, mostly meaningless phrases, snatches of the figments from the past seven days. He became more lucid the closer they came to the pond, and when they reached the mounded bank he was shouting over and over, "He doesn't have the stone!"

Dewlark pushed Vervain over the bank and lost his grip on the wheelchair. It braked mid-slide and tossed Vervain toward the pond, where he sat up and saw first a coil of desiccated flesh in the grass and then Dwyn, wheezing, bleeding, wounded. Vervain crawled to him. The frog's lip was torn, its eye pierced by the ego's venomous tooth, and one foot was broken. Vervain took as much of Dwyn's head in his lap as he could and caressed his soft rubbery skin. He wished that he had arms enough to hold him.

When Dwyn spoke, his voice was mangled, the taut string snapped. "He'll come for you now."

And then Vervain knew what the coil of flesh was: Carnelian's ego, shriveled and dead. "Better me than you. I'm easily replaceable."

"It's not so difficult for me either. You'll see." Dwyn ribbited, and blood gurgled from deep in his throat and dribbled out his nostrils. "Now I see the ripples that will become the big wave," Dwyn said.

"What wave?"

"The one that flips us off our lily pads and turns us belly up."

"No," Vervain whimpered, and he began to weep.

"Oh yes."

"Dew, run and fetch my bag. Please!"

"Look at my leg: it has not healed. Human solutions for frog problems." Dwyn gave a croak like a tired laugh.

Vervain reached for the pond's magic and grasped, but his hands came up empty. "There's nothing, then? This is it? I'll kill him. I'll kill Carnelian."

"I have no qualms about killing humankind. But this one has power. I tried. He made illusions of himself. My tongue swatted empty air."

"He'll be weak now, without his ego. He's already been punished. He's only afraid. He's only hurt, a damaged man." And there he was, already feeling sorry for Carnelian after all. "Why? Why the frograin again? I told you to leave. I told you they wanted this to stop, that they would kill you. Why?"

"Just a few green clouds left in the sky after the storm."

"But why? What was it all for?"

"The rain was my courtship dance."

"What? I don't understand. There's no one else here. It didn't work."

"It brought you, didn't it?"

Vervain held Dwyn's heavy head into the evening, telling him stories from his past. He told him about the pigeon girl who wove a golden nest, who broke her arm and his heart, and the giantess driven to the precipice of a cliff by a mob of frightened teenagers, and whose death was faked to free her. Vampire snails crawled out of the pond seeking the warmth of a weeping wound, and Dewlark starting kicking them back into the water. He swatted flies from the wounds. He fanned Dwyn with giant ferns, trying to stir the stagnant air. And then, as sunset turned the pond to gold, Dwyn hemorrhaged and filled the bank with his blood. Vervain cried out, and Dewlark wrapped his small arms around as much of Dwyn's broad back as he could, and they held him as he shuddered and ribbited in pain.

"And the crest of the wave comes," Dwyn said, and his heart gave one last flutter before coming to rest, and he was dead.

Dewlark wept, and Vervain pulled him away from the blood and held him until his tears were gone.

Together, they gave Dwyn a water burial. They placed stones inside his mouth and dragged him to the edge of the pond. Vervain disrobed and went into the water, pulling while Dewlark pushed from the bank, first with his hands and then with a fallen branch.

The frog sank into the pond with the sound of water.

***

The following day, the ninth of his illness, Vervain found himself at the edge of the pond near the crumbling fane. He kneeled in its shadow and gagged, wondering how he had gotten there. He retched into the pond water, closing his eyes against the reflection of his strained face and his swollen throat, now so round and discolored he wondered if whatever was inside wouldn't burst through and shatter his whole throat. He was afraid to look at himself, afraid that he would see a stranger, a dark and willful stranger.

But he was only afraid for one moment more, and then he threw up.

Something splashed into the shallows and floated there: a golden green globe with a comma-shaped shadow inside. Vervain lifted it and cradled it in his palms. His throat was contracting, and his head cleared. It was not his ego, but an egg. He had had nothing to worry about all along: most problems are imaginary.

And this was the fabled frogstone. It wasn't a jewel, some frog-shaped gewgaw for merchants to quibble over. It was an egg, and his body had kept it warm until it was ready for the world.

Vervain laughed, relieved and full of wonder, and yet a tear came to his eye when he looked once more at the egg and saw within the makings of a tadpole that would one day sprout tiny legs and lose its tail and crawl onto the bank to feel for the first time the full force of the sun. He missed Dwyn already.

Vervain put the egg back in the shallows. There was still danger. Carnelian was likely hiding somewhere nearby, crouching in the reeds, waiting to strike, watching to see where Vervain had hidden the frogstone. Carnelian would think he stole it for himself. Those bent by their desires never believed that others were not similarly enthralled.

"Cousin, is that you?"

Still on his knees, Vervain wheeled around and found Cousin Cattooth standing under the roof of the old fane.

"Kneeling down in obeisance like the clerics of yesteryear?" He chuckled. "It is safe to say the frog is gone, and the frograin? Well, you did it again. You work wonders, cousin, and I'm glad you've stayed so long. I was wondering if you might not stay longer. We don't have many friends, my wife and I, not close ones, and we do enjoy your company. My wife was just saying. Cousin? Cousin, are you okay? What is that?"

Cousin Cattooth pointed, and Vervain turned to find the egg falling toward the sky, slowly and on no particular path, like a balloon. Vervain pulled it down to the pond again, but it wouldn't stay in the water, as if in disobedience. He remembered Dwyn's quiet confidence and smiled, and the egg floated upward as if to show him that the water was not meant to be water.

Vervain looked down at the water, and the still and stagnant air clung to him like a cloak. The pond was a sky mirror. The air was an ocean. The egg was its new moon.

A better world.

"Gather everyone to the pond," Vervain said, getting to his feet.

"What? Everyone in the village? But the bugs are thick as fog. The ground sucks at my feet. I'll lose a boot, or—"

"Are you in pain, cousin?" Vervain touched his

neck, and Cousin Cattooth touched his own, raw with scratches. "Do you feel haunted by a restless spirit? Do you feel as if nothing is quite in its place?"

"Well." He thought about it. "I didn't have the words, but yes. You're right, as usual. I do."

"Then I think it's time."

"For what?"

"I don't know. Do you trust me?"

"Of course I do, but the others..." He shrugged.

"Just get them down here. Get them to trust me. Do what you can. I think you're ready."

And Vervain hoped he was as well, hoped that he wasn't forcing some willful doom on the village. There was the darkness of hatred and fear in his heart, in all hearts, and the light of love as well. The old pond in his heart was murky and always would be: there was never any way of truly knowing good from evil. There was the only the pond and what he did with it.

The villagers trickled down to the pond in groups of four and five, casting baffled and bemused looks at Vervain, whispering gossip and swatting bugs. Cousin Cattooth corralled them, apologizing and placating them in his long-winded way. Dewlark helped, taking the younger children by hand and pulling lost shoes out of the muck. Vervain kept the giant egg from floating off, though he wasn't sure he had any right to do so. He felt Carnelian's presence nearby like a loose tooth, just beyond reproach, but he never appeared.

"That's everyone," Cousin Cattooth said, "excepting those away on business or adventure, and poor Grandma Sod, too ill even to know her name. She will not budge."

"She'll find a way," Vervain said, and then he let the giant egg go. And as it floated up, he plumbed the depths of the pond for the richest magic, and he found a whole font. He drew it up from down below, from the bedrock and the soil, the bottom ooze, the open water, the weedy shallows, and every molecule of air and water. He held it in his hand like a cup of green tea and poured it out onto the world.

Plop!

The world reflected.

Air transformed to water, water turned to air, and the earth remained in the middle. The pond became a gulf of sky above a pool of water that stretched underground in three long lobes like the leaf of a sassafras tree.

"Let it in!" Vervain cried. "Let it in!"

And for one awful moment, he thought they all would drown, but then they began to change.

Cousin Cattooth grew gills on his neck and began to swim in happy pirouettes. Dewlark shrunk, grabbed a shell, and pulled himself inside, peeking out with eyes on stalks. He would never hold a butcher's knife again, because he only had a foot. The innkeeper dissolved into plankton, and a fish with violet scales darted out of the door of the Egress of the Ingret. Grandma Sod swam out the window of her bedroom, her hands replaced by crawdad claws. One by one, the villagers let the magic in, and they changed. They had fins and gills and webbed feet, tails and scales and the long whirligig legs of a water boatman beetle, and the Village in the Damps was flooded and full.

Only one among them didn't change: Carnelian, who held his breath, but not for long. He was crouching in the horsetail, swiftly becoming even more like a horse's tail. Silky and liquid smooth, the lakeweed caught him like a fisherman's lure, and only later would he come loose and drift to the surface, bloated belly up, his flesh already blooming algae.

Vervain swam to the surface of the pool. A shadow swung over the water, and he looked up. Far above, Dwyn's bleached bones soared all together as a skeleton, one leg still broken. It circled once more and then flew south, disappearing behind scraps of rainclouds. There would be a village awakened in the night by the distant rattle of bones or a city plagued by ghastly bonehail. But they would have to call someone else to banish the bones, because Vervain was running out of air.

A CAMBRIAN VENGEANCE
Ian Ableson

The fish were first, of course. Gliding through velvety pitch-black waters, weaving in and out of the caverns that lay honeycombed just below the surface of that unseen warm utopia, one day they found the few ponds overhead that were to them no more than windows into a hostile world. They shrugged (or would have, if they had shoulders), and returned to the frantic pace of their sunken realm. Occasionally a fish might remember the strange bright portals, and return to the ponds to gaze out into the sky. For a brief moment, the smallest spark of dangerous curiosity would touch upon their mind. But the spark would soon be gone. It is not in the best interest of a fish to wonder at the sky.

The birds found the garden next, for wings are wondrous weapons of transportation. Mallards and owls, kingfishers and robins, one by one they all came to rest in the garden. The garden served a different purpose for them than it did for the fish—it was not quite a home, perhaps, but a sanctuary on the airborne journeys that dominated their lives. In the garden there was food and shelter and no predators to be found. As generations passed, each successive flock would pause long migrations to show the garden to their young, so that it might continue to serve as a haven for them and their offspring after them.

Perhaps it would have been best if it had stayed that way, as a dream for fish and a respite for birds. But it was not meant to be; change is inevitable.

It is difficult to pinpoint exactly when it

happened. Before long, after a moment, in due time, before it was meant to, eventually, suddenly—the fish don't much care to dwell on time, and the birds were never asked. Nevertheless, some entrance that had previously been closed off was opened, and earthbound creatures found the garden at last. Almost overnight, tranquility and silence were replaced by hooves and scales and swiftly sprinting paws. The changes these new creatures affected on the garden were far more drastic than any that the birds and fish could have managed. Zigzags of trails were cleared all across the landscape, connecting the watery domains of the fish to the newly-crafted dens of the land animals. Their homes showed astonishing variety; they dug deep twisting burrows in the earth, they lived in fallen trees and patches of brush, they flattened the grasses and slept together in massive herds. The birds watched all of this, and they were uneasy, even if they had no word for the feeling. For the most part, the land animals did not openly antagonize the birds or the fish, being content to prey on vegetation or amongst themselves. A few of the more enterprising birds—the hawks and the owls being the most prominent—even learned to take advantage of the sudden presence of land-bound meat. After a brief period of chaos as the garden struggled to resolve the new food web, equilibrium was reached again.

Perhaps this is where it should have stopped.

Humans appeared. There was more to the story than that, but as far as the birds and the fishes and the land animals were concerned, it was the result that mattered. Humans appeared with all of their complexity. They changed the landscape even more dramatically than the creatures of hooves and paws. They cleared vast tracts of forest to make room for huge, bizarre structures that they built from materials they dredged out of the earth—some of these stretched so high that they even invaded the realms of the birds.

Humans crafted boats and sailed over the windows of the fishes. The paths they created through the landscape were far wider than the body-width trails made by the creatures of hooves and paws. The animals were bewildered. What sort of new creature was this that had come to their garden? For a long time, the animals avoided making contact with the humans and only watched them from afar, but this did little to reassure them. It seemed that every passing day brought new oddities. Humans played games not to teach their young to survive, but for no apparent reason other than to pass the time. Food gathered by one human was shared among many, regardless of kinship. Even the humans' mating rituals (a set of rules that, until that point, the animals thought they did understand), were entirely beyond their comprehension.

And the sound! Humans were so loud! They spoke freely and sometimes even sang a strange music, and they did so without fear of predation. At all times of day or night there would be murmuring, yelling, and laughter coming from the humans in the garden. Even the songbirds and the frogs were never so persistent in their desire to communicate.

Nevertheless, despite their oddities, over time the animals felt themselves drawn to these strange new creatures. The horses, those proud and regal masters of the plains, were first to come out from hiding and approach the humans. A bond was formed between the horses and the new beings that, to this day, and in spite of all that would come afterwards, would never truly be broken. As the other animals saw the growing kinship of horses and men, they too approached humans in trust. For a while, it was an idyllic time of learning and companionship.

Here. Here, with the benefits bestowed by hindsight, it is easy to definitively say it should have stopped.

But then something else changed. None of the

beasts ever knew for certain what event served as the catalyst for humanity's metamorphosis. Some of the more observant creatures suspected the snakes might have known something, but they were not forthcoming with the tale. All the animals knew was that suddenly the mindset of the humans shifted entirely; they were more calculating and more pragmatic, and their attitudes towards the beasts of land and air and water became ruthless. They pulled the fish from the water with nets and hooks until the window to the sky became a gateway to oblivion. They took birds from the air using cunning new constructs, raided their nests and stole their eggs, and mangled their trees to create even more ludicrously elaborate structures. But the land animals had it the worst. They were corralled and hunted and ridden, and the bonds of companionship that they'd enjoyed with the humans dwindled to nothingness for all but a few select species. The humans claimed huge swathes of land for themselves, and all thoughts of sharing this land with their fellow animals, or indeed even with each other, quickly vanished. The humans fought amongst themselves nearly as much as they antagonized the other creatures, and the aftermath of their conflicts scarred the land. The garden became nearly unrecognizable. And the speed! It happened so quickly! Even those animals who managed to hide from the humans or to fight back against them had no chance to adapt to the new environment, as good homes and sources of food vanished in the blink of an eye.

Something had to be done, of course; all the creatures of the garden knew this. Such actions will always produce predictable reactions. But the creatures of land were far too bewildered, too busy fleeing to the few parts of the garden that they felt they could still call their own to rally against humanity. The birds, meanwhile, chose avoidance; they took to the skies and stayed higher in the trees, abandoning the world below to humanity's madness.

Which left the fish. It is easy to underestimate the fish. But they are older than anything else that lives, and their realm is that of the deepest and darkest parts of the world, where light and air are nothing but dreams. Once the fish had determined their course, there was no hesitation.

They swam down, down, down, deep into the depths of the earth, deeper than any of their kind had ever dared to go. They dove so deep that they reached the places where chill water was replaced by fire and liquid stone. There, in the deepest catacombs of the darkest seas, far below the point that any living thing might be expected to dwell, they created a place of punishment for the humans. It was an abyss, a place of pain and torment, and it served as both retribution and threat. Upon death, humans would be judged. Of this the fish were sure. And those that were judged unfavorably would spend the rest of eternity in this new place of punishment. Once it was made, this inevitable place of reaction, it filled a void in the world. It balanced out the equation, restoring the natural equilibrium. The fish were satisfied, and so they left their creation to the depths and returned to more hospitable waters.

The fish were first, of course. And one day, after the trumpets sound, after the world turns to fire and floods, the fish will be last as well. They know this. They are patient.

They will wait.

RIVER VESSEL
LaVa Payne

None of which is to say that the soft underbelly was not apparent. It was. It floundered on the shorelines long after... and we waited, wondering if it would return soon.

But the wall of water did not return, and so much of all life rushed ahead each moment in the sparse thought. The water wall would return.

So much of the cabbage and turnips were over-picked, and the koi danced in between the scattered petals of the water.

Shey-shon had waited with her basket draped like medium silk over a bolt of fabric. Her eyes were searching the cliff's jagged jaw hoping for the silhouette of his return.

But unlike the waves on the shoreline, he did not offer his many happy returns. A fisherman was a gambler on the ocean.

When setting off from the bamboo pier, each pontiff became an abacus bead capable of being added to or removed from the fishing village. It was a calculated risk that Shey-shon had known of her long promised love.

Swift and careless she dropped her red orchid. When the water arose once again, the waves would carry her promise to love Duyun-tai wherever he found refuge now—even if it was clenched to the Tsunami's breast of pearl and wine.

NANT'SEVE
ASSAGESDE
UCHTHECR
DOMINION
LECTADARK
LANDMALCO
TMENTBLAC
SNUDESHU

II

TERATOMA
PANORAMA

FOR THE HIDDEN WOMAN
Virginia Chase Sutton

—from The Garden of Earthly Delights
—after Hieronymus Bosch

Beneath an enormous pale yellow leaf
she rests, belly down, breathing clean
fresh dirt. She promises nothing more.
I am a child lurking beneath banks
of untamed lilac bushes blossoming

along the perimeter of the backyard.
Such lovely colors—pink, white,
lavender—reach aimlessly towards
the sun, taller than a man. It is where
I burrow, my shell cracked open by

my father who will not leave me. But
this woman, curvy perfection and long
legs, sleeps easily, almost out of sight.
Around her buttocks and upper thighs
are shimmering bands of jewels, such

adornment in row after row. Does she
entice men with each dip and shimmy
her body makes? Above, out of sight,
a finger points, as if tempting her
to wake and urge her back, back though

she is clearly done. Yet the hand slips
towards her, signaling for good or evil,
the way my father creeps into my bedroom,
into the bed we share for so long. I am
tired, wish to sleep in night's dark corners,

not to raise my gown to his open palms.
I can barely see. She and I are the same
though she is an adult, and we are
exhausted from too much love and quest
for soft flesh. *I want, I want* she speaks

though no one hears. *I want, I want* I echo.
No one listens, no one saves us. Selected
whether it is *yes* or *no*. Our desires in
differing times, languages and places,
somehow too similar never to be heard.

NEW WORLD FRUIT
Tiffany Morris

I. Pastoral

Anemone scales
cloud and scrapes peony tar
from peeling daylight.

Feather and scale fall
petal soft to whispering
grasses, singing pools.

Pricked fingers tongue flesh
ripe fruit hanging picked dropping
eager skin on skin.

A fish eye staring
into sky and open mouth
grass and ground and grave–

II.   Trilling

Palepale the flesh the
wet soak[ing] tubers the flesh
quiver[ing] bloom[ing]

Crushbeak dappledskin
on tongue berrysoft crush[ing]
tearing meatbone squeak

Meat is meat is meat
tartsong biting clear sing[ing]
meat is flesh is meat

Wormblood chunkblood salt
tearing snapright bones apart
mansongs chirp[ing] LOUD

III.   Extinction

Tendril and vine sway:
volcano, mountain yawn[ing]
scraped blue scraped blue scraped—

Ghostly the horn bends
into water: drink[ing] cold.
Cave and hoof, heartbeat–

Plume and tube, bloom[ing]
limb and leaf scrawled across green:
tusk tearing at sun.

Antler shed, growling.
Tree bark [and fur falls quiet].
Eyes / witness / towers.

BOSCHIARY
Frederick L. Shiels

Only thing better than a walk
through the garden of delights
is a glide-through at low altitude
on acid, weed, or tequila poured on ice.

But make no mistake, unless
this glide-through can be pulled off
invisibly, it's just not worth disturbing anyone.

    I.   A circle of nudes—and clothing is rare here—
          are seated and bent under one giant strawberry,
          not unlike Woodstock without mud and guitars.

    II.   A soft-eyed fish looks on through bare branches,
          tail curled like a mermaid's and held
          up by knights. Nothing,

    III. I mean nothing is simple here.
          The gentlest of sex is everywhere,
          medieval Kama Sutra with a twist.

    IV. But mostly demureness rules the scene.
          Exotic birds and berries large and moist
          are the toys the painter favors for his lovers.

V.   Everywhere creatures real and imagined serve
        as props—
    Long-haired unicorns, roosters, creepy crawly
        fauna
    convincing extinct species from Darwinian
        chains.

VI.   Bosch's sorcerer's brush has seen fit to place
    small pallid gray observers of the revelry,
    as if not entitled to the fun.

VII.   And everywhere from outside one imagines,
        noisy
    conversations like at any festival or party.
    So the silence haunts the viewer of the canvas.

VIII. It has haunted them for five hundred years
        or more.
    And so the dream of walking into the sounds
        and smells
    of this vast place, circus of stolid van Aken,

IX.   lives on for some, and somewhere he must be
        laughing
    at all the things we do not, cannot know.

A PAINT OF VIEW
Dr. Jackie Ferris

I

Magdalena's head was bowed as she scurried through the narrow streets. Thin, tapered houses flaking with cracked paint towered above her like giant fingers. They blocked out the light but offered little shelter from the hard rain. It was the first they had had for five months. The long, hot summer had started in early May, shortly after Easter. Its relentless heat meant that everything was rank with human effluent flowing from open sewers. It was a paradise for fat-bellied rats who feasted idly in the stinking streets. The choking steam rising from the cobblestones made the obnoxious smells worse.

Magdalena, like King Felipe 11, her lord and master, blamed the Moroccan Arabs—known locally as Moriscos—for Spain's problems. Following their revolt in the south in 1569, he had ordered their dispersal from Granda. Many of them had sought refuge in the villages near Madrid. There they could afford neither food nor shelter. Twenty-two years later their makeshift camps still straddled the mountainsides. Every day the Moriscos flooded the nearby towns in search of work and nourishment. Their continued presence spread mistrust among the villagers who shunned and looked down on them.

High on the mountainside, the King's palace—the Escorial—stood serenely above their filth and misgivings. A bastion of wealth and power, it was intended to remind everyone that the Spanish throne was at the centre of the Counter Reformation, and a fitting burial place for Felipe's father, the Holy Roman Emperor. For the dispossessed it was a constant aide-mémoire to the unattainability of wealth. They had no idea of the paranoia and fragility that such riches were built on. Felipe's failure to sort out trivia from important information paralysed the Court. Their atrophy had led to Spain's economic stagnation.

Hurrying through the streets Magdalena was painfully aware of how bad that stagnation was. She pulled her shawl tighter around her scrawny body; even her bones felt damp. With a determined effort she increased her pace, then groaned as she slipped on a pile of human shit.

The rats ignored her as she got to her feet but the people pushed and shoved as they tried to pass. Fighting her shame she glanced around, searching for something to clean her stained leather slippers. There was nothing but shit and rats and already she was late. The King's head chef was sleeping off a hangover. Afraid to do anything without his authorisation the palace bakers had tasked Magdalena with buying the best bread in town. Even the idea filled her with dread. The all too familiar feeling was a living epitaph to her existence. Her mother, an unhappy and angry woman, constantly berated her. Her father was mostly a distant drunken figure who appeared only to rape her in the name of God. It had begun ten years ago, when she was four. Incestuous rape was not uncommon in the palace, and as a scullery maid she could hope for nothing but more abuse.

She cast her head upwards towards the grim mountains of Guadarrama, looming in front of her. Cloaked in grey granite they reminded her of the man-made façade of the Escorial. Spain, her country, belonged to men, not women, yet it was withering in an economic decline. The King and his men had lost the Netherlands and their ineptitude had caused the

Granada uprising. To assuage their mood the courtiers discussed the brave new worlds of the Americas and its treasures. In reality there was little evidence of that wealth in the palace. King Felipe 11, a staunch Catholic, feared Protestant revolution more than he feared God. Locally, he was known as Felipe the Prudent and Defender of the Faith. Within the palace walls he was known as the Faithful Ditherer. She sighed: the duplicity of the Catholic faith had much to answer for. It denied pleasure and yet allowed her father to satiate his own, at his will. In Felipe's Court men did what their conscience bade them, and, thanks to the much used confessional boxes, their conscience was as fickle as their prayers.

Magdalena shivered and almost tripped again as an Arab man nudged her as he passed. The musky smell of his cologne lingering in his wake was a welcome relief. Regaining her balance she watched him saunter down the street. Suddenly he turned and winked. She felt her cheeks turn crimson but he was too far away to see. Yet somehow, even from this distance, she caught his gaze. He was looking at her with interest, not lust, as he beckoned her towards him. She hesitated—no one had ever shown interest in her before; she was merely an object.

Charmed, and instantly forgetting about the bread, she rushed towards him. He turned, nodding in the direction of an even narrower path leading up a hill. She wished that the shit around her ankles would disappear as she quickened her step. When she finally reached him she was out of breath.

He did not speak but dropped to the ground, splattering her in a cloud of dust. As it cleared, his brown, deer-like eyes stared back at her, making her cower.

"Do not be afraid, we are well met."

Magdalena folded her arms. "Met, we do not know each other."

"Do the birds not sing in the sky as the sun breaks through? Then so are we." His voice was soft, almost like a caress.

"What do you want of me?" She felt that she was stripped of her skin and he could see into her.

"Daughter of Christ, I seek that which is not of this world but lies within it. You hold the key to that."

"Are you mad? I am nought but a scullery maid."

"Madness is made sane by those who understand it. I am who I am."

"You speak in riddles. I should not even be here; your dress tells me that you are a Morisco."

"Dress does define the man. I am forbidden to speak my native tongue yet I can dress as I please."

"You speak the tongue that is mine and of our great King Felipe."

"Castilian is the language of my birth, not of my heart."

"And your heart would define your country?"

"Heart defines my being. In the future, Granda will define Spain; its heritage is Arabic, not Castilian. Your Nordic Kings do not know the heart and passion that belongs to the south, nor the gypsy music and dancing that lifts the soul."

"Your words spread confusion, not truth. Why did you bring me here?"

"It is your feet, not I, that summoned you."

She shook her head. "You are a sorcerer, you have bewitched me."

"I am who I am. It is you who have yet to become yourself.' "

"You speak with the forked tongue of the devil."

"It is not the tongue that carries the devil's work; it is the mind that interprets it." Magdalena watched, transfixed as he pulled out a paper filled with herbs and put it in his mouth. His eyes stayed on her as he struck a stone against a rock to spark. He lit the rolled up paper and then drank deeply from it before passing it to her. "Try it; then you will know a world you cannot."

"Felipe has forbidden a Spaniard to talk with a Morisco. I cannot take it."

"Yet you talk to me."

"I am bewitched."

"The truth is often beguiling." He offered her the rolled paper again.

She put her hands up. "No, I cannot take it."

"Then why do you speak with me?" He handed her the lit paper. "Take it and you will rid the shackles of this stinking world."

"Your sorcery is false."

"First try, and then judge."

She stared at him wondering why she had followed him. There was something about his eyes. It was the first time that anyone had looked at her as a person, not a thing. Unable to hold his gaze, she took the paper from him and then drew on it the way he had.

In front of her, the granite mountains shimmered in fuzzy waves of light. She blinked as the sheep on the distant mountain merged with the rock. Below her people sprouted like green shoots from the olive trees that dotted the mountainside. "This is witchcraft. What have you done to me?"

He grinned back at her. "Unlocked a world that you cannot see, yet it exists all around us. We are blinded by the light."

She pulled the paper from her mouth. "Here, take it, it is the devil's work." She handed the herb-filled paper back to him, struggling not to laugh. Unicorns were dropping from the sky through golden waterfalls and dragons, breathing fire, were flying on chariots of white clouds.

"You are too quick to praise the devil." He raised an eyebrow.

"Nay, I am slow and bewitched. My mother will have my head when I return. She will see the devil in my eyes."

"Then you believe in God?"

"God? I spoke of the devil." She looked at him puzzled.

"There can be no god without the devil—evil begets good, and good begets evil."

"You can't say that good is stained by evil."

He took a final draw then threw the rolled paper onto the ground. "Without good there would be no evil."

Magdalena shook her head. It was hard to accept but his ideas were enticing.

"Close your eyes." Magdalena jumped. His words weren't coming from his lips—they were erupting from inside of her. "You can see unicorns and dragons yet they do not exist."

"The ancients said they did." She wasn't sure if the words had slipped out of her head or she had said them.

"But you have never seen a book. You do not know what unicorns look like. Your imagination cannot conjure up creatures without some basis in fact."

She took a sharp intake of breath. "Perhaps not but they were as real as you or I."

"Believe me when I tell you that you have entered another world."

Magdalena opened her eyes and then looked up. Dark grey clouds were amassing in the sky but she could still see the dragons and the unicorns. "Why tell me this?"

He let the silence fall between them for a moment before answering. "You are from the palace."

"How do you know that?"

"The man who calls himself the King of Spain has spies everywhere. He is not the only one, we too have our sources. A painting was delivered to the

Escorial a few days ago; it tells the story of the true sorcerer yet the Christians claim that it is the story of Creation and the Fall."

"Then the Christians are right—our King is the Defender of the Faith.'

"Perhaps so, but the painting has little to do with faith." His long mane of hair rippled through the air like a black river as he shook his head. "Yet there are those who are blind that think it does."

"What do you mean? The King is the owner; the painting must celebrate the true faith."

"Then faith is blind. The painting proves it. It has three panels. When the front two are open they reveal rich treasures inside. On the two front panels is a crystal sphere half-filled with water. Perhaps it is the earth viewed only by a being that lives in the starry skies."

"Only God lives in the heavens."

"How can we know, if we have not been there?"

She shook her head. "What has that got to do with me?"

"Everything."

She put her head in her hands. "This is witchcraft. I am nothing but a stupid scullery maid; the heavens are of no interest to me."

"You recognised me in the street. You thought it was I who brought you here but it is you who summoned me. You have the power, not me."

Magdalena rubbed her eyes—the unicorns and dragons were fading but her head ached. "Please, do not try to trick me. You made me follow you."

He tilted his head as an owl hooted. "Did you hear that? The owl rarely breaks the bonds of darkness. It's a sign."

"It means the devil is at work."

"Or the sorcerer." The look of disbelief in her eyes made him add: "You do not have to believe me; Felipe's painting proves it. You must see it. Once you do, everything will change. It holds the truth."

She laughed. "Now I know that you jest. I am nothing more than a scullery maid. I am not permitted to go near the King's quarters. I would never be allowed to look at the painting. You know this, and that is why you dally with my mind."

He shook his head. "You will find a way—you must. Within you is the key that unlocks a time when our gods did not exist. Men created the stories of God. Men, in the name of God, are responsible for many bad things. It is our, no, your duty, to return our world to a world without gods."

An image of her father flitted into her head. "Men are the root of all evil. That I can believe, but I am a simple scullery maid, what can I do to change anything?" She repeated her mantra.

"It is your destiny, you will find a way. First, you must return to the palace and look at the painting. It will tell you what to do."

"How? I am rarely permitted to leave the scullery. They do not allow scullery maids anywhere near the King's quarters."

"The palace let you come to the village."

"The King needed bread."

"The vessel towards truth is not important; I will guide you. You found me once, you will find me again. I come from the world of the painting, not this world." They both turned as the owl hooted. "Look for me there, but not in human form. Remember, Magdalena, you do not come from here, you come from there."

There. Where did he mean, the painting? She tried to compose her thoughts. It was hard to concentrate because of the fuzziness in her eyes. She rubbed them and then gasped. She was standing in the middle of a street in front of the bakers. The Arab man was nowhere to be seen. She glanced at her ankle—the shit had gone. Had she dreamt the whole thing?

A woman nudged her in the back. "Come on, carino, it's your turn, are you moving or what? You might not need the bread but we do."

Magdalena turned towards the wizened old shrew behind her. "How long have I been here?"

"Since the morning sun tipped over the mountains and clothed us in daylight."

She turned away from the woman to glance at the long queue stretching past the narrow street and into another. It was impossible that she could have been anywhere else. "Sorry, I was daydreaming."

"You can't do that when there is bread to be had."

Magdalena nodded—she must have been there all the time but the images in her mind were more real than where she was standing.

"Are you moving or not?" The woman was losing her temper as she pushed her harder. Magdalena shuffled inside the bakery then put her hands to her eyes as the heat from the hot oven fires hit her.

"What can I get you, my lovely?" The large, big-bellied man in the apron smiled at her lustfully. His countenance reminded her of her father.

"A dozen sticks of bread and forty buns, please."

He ran his hands down his apron-clad, rotund belly. "That is a large order from someone so thin. I have all these people behind you to feed; such an order will make it impossible. Would you deny the people food?"

"It is the King that demands it, not I."

The man rubbed his pink arthritic hands together. "Then we must grant him his wishes although he cares not for ours."

"The King must care for the country. It is his duty."

"And is this land not made up of his people?"

She shrugged. "We are who we are."

"People are expendable; it is the gold and the jewelled sacrifices taken in the name of God to convert the pagan savages in the Americas that he cares for. Like them, we are but pawns on his chessboard, fashioned in God's name."

Magdalena sighed. "Are not my golden ducats as good as the rest?"

The baker grinned as he scooped them up in his hand. "Better than most because they come straight from the Treasury. I will give you what I have; most of the people in the line behind you come with hope and promise in their eyes, not golden ducats. But where is your basket? With an order of this size, it will be filled to the top."

Fear masked her eyes; in her haste to flee the palace she had forgotten it. "It has escaped me. My mind was tied up with other things, not bread."

"It is a strange mind that does not care to feed itself. But you are fortunate: I have a basket made from reeds from the lake. It will cost you as much as the bread. Without the basket, you cannot carry the bread and there I will make my killing."

Magdalena nodded, knowing that her mother would scold and whip her when she returned to the Escorial for her imprudence. "Robbed by my foolishness I must buy it. What choice do I have?"

"None, nor do the people who must wallow in the King's pleasure of poverty. Let your basket be a reminder—one day we must all pay the price for our misdeeds." He piled the bread and buns into the basket as he spoke, then handed it to her.

***

As she hurried back to the palace she re-ran the conversation with the Arab in her head. She must have dreamt it. It was impossible to be in two places at once; besides, she didn't even know his name.

"Who gives you the right to pass?" The guard's question interrupted her thoughts.

She looked up, surprised to see that she was standing in front of the servants' entrance to the palace. "The King's bread. If I don't hurry, it will be cold; already I have dallied too long."

"Aye, and the bread is not only cold, it's wet. You should have covered them, lass." He shook his head as he let her pass.

Chastised, Magdalena dashed into the scullery and laid them by the hot fire, hoping to dry them before anyone could see.

Seconds later, her mother burst through the big oak door leading to the kitchen. "What are you doing?" Magdalena cowered as her mother continued to scold her. "You should have been back hours ago. The King is livid. He has had to eat meat without bread for his breakfast." Her mother picked up one of the soggy scones. "What is this?"

"The bread, mother."

"Surely you cannot expect the King to eat this?"

"The poor begging on the streets would kill for it."

She slapped her daughter's face. "You will join them if you cannot make this bread good. The King will not suffer such pickings." She turned on her heel as Magdalena picked up another soggy bun yet the Arab's words filled her with confidence; suddenly the bread no longer mattered.

"Have you heard about the painting?"

"What?" Her mother yelled back at her. "You don't have time for paintings, concentrate on the bread. It is only the bread that saves you from a whipping."

Magdalena took a toasting fork and pushed a bread bun nearer the fire then winced as her mother's fingernails dug into her shoulder. She swung her around, making her drop the bread; she watched it spin along the dusty floor.

"Where did you hear about the painting? It only arrived here a few days ago. You are not allowed to speak to the King's personal servants, so who told you?" She pulled a face as she made a sign of the cross. "Don't tell me you were stupid enough to speak to someone outside?"

Magdalena tried to think as she picked up the bread bun and rubbed it on her skirt. "I had to speak to the baker."

"And he told you about the painting?"

"The whole town is talking about it."

"What are they saying?" She scratched the scab on her face, making it bleed.

"That it is the work of the devil and the King is bewitched by it."

Her mother raised a scraggy eyebrow. "They say the same here. By all accounts, it is a blasphemous piece of witchcraft."

"Have you seen it?"

"No, nor would I want to—the devil lives in it, everyone says so. The King keeps it on the floor in his office; apparently he looks upon it for hours."

"In his office! But I thought paintings were to hang on walls."

"The role of paintings is not your concern." She stared at her daughter suspiciously. "Why the interest?"

"You said it, the devil is in it. Everyone is afraid of it in town; the baker said no good would come of it."

"And no good will come of the bread and the buns if you don't dry them out; enough of this mindless chatter, it is the devil's work. Hurry, lass, the cook will have my bones for soup when he wakes up and finds that the King has no bread."

Her mother slammed the heavy oak door as Magdalena began the task of drying the buns but it was hard to concentrate. Her mind was overflowing with ideas. If there really was a painting, she must have seen and talked to the Morisco. No one else in the town had mentioned it. Somehow, she had to find a way into the King's quarters; it was the only way she would know the truth. First, she had to dry the buns.

Time passed slowly, then just as she was about to finish, she heard the stomp of her father's footsteps. Dread replaced her feeling of boredom as he yelled: "Magdalena."

She got to her feet hoping that a kiss and a cuddle would suffice but the smell of whisky on his breath and the lust in his eyes suggested that it would not. "Papa, please don't." She backed off towards the fire, feeling its heat burning her legs.

"Come here, girl, I have needs that must be met." He dragged her towards him then lowered his breeches as he threw her to the ground. His flaming red penis was throbbing as he took it in his hands and thrust it into her. She winced, trying not to cry out; that would increase his desire; instead, she tried to think of something else. It was impossible as her father's weight bore down on her. She tried to relax, knowing her own tension made it worse, but her muscles tightened as he ripped into her; thrusting his body again and again into her. Then suddenly he rolled over. His fat white stomach, bulging through his waistcoat reminded her of the lard the chef used to fry the stake bread she was given. The perspiration poured from his red face and his body stank of stale, unwashed sweat and clothes.

She dared not move until he had stood up and headed towards the outside door. She heard him open it and then piss against the wall.

The back door banged shut. As she got to her feet his shadow hovered over her. "Clean that up when I leave." He pointed to the outside. "My piss smells. It must be you, you dirty whore. If I catch anything, I will kill you." He made the sign of the cross then spit on the ground. "The devil takes care of his own; that is where you came from, his fiery lair of damnation. Your witchcraft makes me do these things; I pray that God protects me from your spells."

She waited until he had left before she gathered a pan of hot water and scrubbing brush and took it outside. It wasn't just the wall she wanted to clean, nor was it simply her body. If she could get rid of her cluttered thoughts, she might find out who she really was. If the painting existed, then she could begin her journey of discovery.

II

The cold dampness seeped through the scullery floor into Magdalena's clothes. She had not slept. The clock in the kitchen struck every hour on the hour. She could not count but earlier the strikes were more frequent and then there were fewer. Now, each hour, there were more. Soon it would be pre-dawn and the palace would begin to stir. If she was going to see the painting she had to move.

She jumped up from the floor and dusted herself down. Except for a few rats nibbling their way across the floor, she was alone. Tiptoeing, she ventured into the kitchen. There were more rats chewing scraps on the kitchen table but they ignored her as she made her way across the hallway and up the first flight of stairs to where the King's servants slept. She had visited her parent's room on a few, rare occasions. Her father was a manservant to one of the King's equerry and they had been given a small room befitting their status. Each bedroom door was locked tight as she stole her way along the passageway towards a slightly larger flight of stairs. Quietly, she made her way upwards, then gasped. The light flooding in through glass windows that flanked the long corridor was like a magical stream of moonlight. She had never seen windows before but now she knew that they could magnify light. Unable to resist, she ran towards one and put her hands on the cool glass. Below her, the monks made their way through the cloisters for matins. She was ignorant of most of the palace life but it was common knowledge that the King joined them once matins was over and the dawn light was breaking. Soon the guards would be awake, wanting their breakfasts before they began their duties of protecting the King.

Fear shot through her. Was she too late? She turned away from the window and ran along the passageway. She had come too far to turn back. The next flight of stairs was much grander. The candle lights were flickering as she made her way up them. Then, as she turned the corner from the marble staircase, she froze. Two guards stood like statues in front of a door. For a moment she wondered if it was the King's bedroom but it was too close to the kitchen smells. The guards were staring straight ahead. They would not see her if she moved slowly. She pressed her body into the wall and crept shadow-like along the hallway to the next staircase.

Stealthily, she climbed the marble steps, expecting more guards on the next floor. If they spotted her they would kill her. An owl hooted as she reached the top. She stopped, remembering the Morisco's words. The sound of raised voices and the pounding of running feet collided with her heart, hammering against her ribs. She tried to listen. The men were running away from her, up another flight of stairs; something or someone had sparked their alarm. As their footsteps grew fainter the owl hooted again. Taking it as a good omen, she continued into the hallway. It was much grander and seemed to stretch towards infinity. She strained her eyes as the hallway narrowed. She could barely make out the backs of the guards as they ran up steps at the far end of the hall.

To her right there were lots of doors; it was impossible to guess which one was the King's office. Leading off to her left were windows looking on to the courtyard below. The hallway was wide and well-lit by candlelight casting strange shadows across the walls. Magdalena smiled as she spotted the shadow of an owl. It hovered across one of the doorways. She ran towards it.

Her hands trembled as she wrapped them around the large brass handle and pushed the door open. A sliver of moonlight cut through the darkness. She could see the King's desk and beyond it, the painting glowing in the silvery shaft of light. Mesmerized, she moved towards it. Just as the Morisco had said, the painting was closed and the wooden panels were adorned with a crystal sphere. It had a ghostly, other-world appearance. God was in the top left-hand corner reading a book. Was the crystal sphere God's creation or was he merely reading about its creation? The book was open; there was an inscription: *For he spoke, and it came to be, he commanded, and it stood firm.*

She re-read it. Did this mean the Morisco was wrong and the painting was about faith? She hesitated before, slowly, she reached out and opened the wooden panels to reveal the painting within the painting. The colour blinded her. Strange, high pitched noises assaulted her. Putting her hands to her ears she tried to block the wailing. It was useless; the sounds were coming from her.

She stepped back, trying to ignore the howling as she studied the brightly coloured images. Everything about the painting, with its three different panels, was strange: strange beautiful, strange odd. The colours fizzled with so much life it was hard to concentrate on the details. The first panel showed Adam and Eve. God was creating them. She peered closer. There was something troubling about the scene. In the forefront, there was a birthing pool for animals. All kinds of creatures that she had never seen before were emerging from it. The three humanoid figures were above them. To the left of Adam, a strange-looking cat had a dead animal in its mouth. Death did not exist in paradise.

She tried not to think—it was easy. The pink and blue colours were mesmerising. God was pink, the colour modern artists used to show innocence. Why had the painter painted God as innocent? Was he innocent of the fate of man? How did she even know this? Her thoughts perplexed her almost as much as the painting. How could she think such thoughts? Colour, like thought, had never interested her. Her clothes were drab castoffs yet now she had opinions about colour as well as paintings and theology. She moved closer, magnetised, as pinks and blues flowed out of the painting like a rainbow of fingers, drawing her into it.

Finally, the rivers of colour stopped. Everything was clear. The figures of God, and Adam and Eve were in front of her. As she looked up at them the realisation that she was in the painting hit her. She glanced downwards. Her body was covered with fine brown hair. The body of a scullery maid, overlooked and abused, had disappeared; now it was a rabbit's body, gazing on God.

Adam was lying on the grass, his toes were touching Christ; it was the figure of Christ, not God the Father, she could see that now. Not only was the figure pink and innocent, he was too young to be God. Christ was indifferent to Adam's gaze as he had his hand firmly on Eve's arm. It was impossible to know where one figure stopped and the other began. Whoever this man-god-like figure was, it was man's creation, not God's.

Shifting her gaze she turned her attention to the cat with the dead bird dangling from its mouth. It was close to Adam—death was close to new life. She swallowed hard, trying not to breathe in the scent of death. This was the Garden of Eden before the Fall. *Nothing was what it seemed.* She heard her mind filtering through the colour of blue. Blue paint was an expensive colourant made from the gemstone of lapis lazuli. Why had the painter lavished it on the lake and the mountains behind the human figures, and not Christ? How did she even know about blue?

The blue was playing havoc with her thoughts. She shivered, but not physically, because she could not move. Her long floppy ears were pinned against her back. She could hear the water in the lake and the splatter of water from the strange pink fountain that rose from the green pasture land in front of the grazing elephant. Elephant! King Felipe would have liked that because it represented the Christian crusade. Looking around she was not sure what else he would have cared for.

The birds, whirling into an open-mouthed feature behind the elephant, were escaping from a hole in one edifice, directly into another. The Circle of Life: distilled from broken birth eggs, or boredom from an inability to break free? It was impossible to tell.

Yet if this was the Garden of Eden, some things were almost consistent. The Tree of Life, laden with apples, had sprouted from the Garden of Eden. There was only one visible tree. It had no apples hanging from its branches, only green, palm-like cactus fronds, stretching upwards. Behind Adam and Eve stood a pink fountain adorned with fruit. She was looking straight at it. At the base of the fountain, an owl peered through a round hole.

Are you the Morisco? A thought struggled out of her head.

An owl is defined by its breed, not its land.

Her thought bounced back. *It is a creature of the night. Do you beget evil or knowledge?*

Evil is in the head of he that thinks it; as is knowledge. Both flow from the same source.

She glanced at the cat. *Death is not supposed to exist in paradise.*

But death is part of life—to die we must live, and to live we must die.

Our Lord, Jesus Christ, died on the cross to save us from death.

Then how shall we live if we cannot die?

She glanced at the figure of Christ between Adam and Eve. He should not be there. He wasn't even born.

Behind her, she sensed, but could not see, a smaller tree laden with fruit. A snake coiled around its trunk. Its ability to shed its skin meant rebirth yet the Bible conferred on it the evil powers of Satan, not resurrection.

Her thoughts jumbled at the contradiction. She needed to get out but she was painted to the spot. She tried to imagine how she might move as the colours began to blur. Images cascaded into one another then suddenly she spotted Adam clutching a strawberry—the symbol of brief Hedonistic pleasure. He was offering it to Eve. Was it Adam, not Eve, who was responsible for their fall from grace? In front of them, the owl looked on, clearly unhappy that the chain of events was already in process. Fate and its inevitability were wandering ahead of them. She understood that now that she was in the second panel.

Its newness frightened her. The fruit—known as forbidden in the land she had just come from, the first panel—was everywhere. Fish walked on land, and birds and shells had humans in their mouths. Some couples sat in bubbles, others cavorted. Was this God's world or man's?

You don't have to come to me, we can exchange thoughts.
Thoughts?
You are receiving me, aren't you?
Magdalena wished that she could nod. *Who are you?*
I am who I am. We met in the village.
The Morisco?
To name me is to know me.
I spoke to a man, not an owl.
You exchanged thoughts with an owl in the other panel. You are a rabbit, does that make you less a woman?
She looked down at her fur. *Is this really me?*
Our form is irrelevant. Time changes how we look; a painting can do the same.
But I am not older, I am a rabbit.

It is you who says it.

The fur and ears do prove it. But I do not feel it.

Then are you still Magdalena even though you look like a rabbit?

I feel like me but I must confess, I no longer look like me.

And is the spirit derived by the way we look?

Time can cast its stain on who we are. As a child, I thought as a child. But I now am a rabbit, yet I do not think as such, and you are an owl yet you speak like a Morisco.

Morisco or human? You are in the painting. Can you really still say that looks define who we are?

I cannot believe I am here, it is some trickery of yours. I am dreaming and will soon wake up on the scullery floor.

Who knows what the dawn will bring. Now you are here and your outer shape is that of the rabbit.

Both the rabbit and owl are creatures of witchcraft.

Some say that the rabbit is lucky; others that it holds the key to the underworld. The owl is a bird of wisdom and a bird of death; it stalks the night's skies, not the daylight. It knows the ways of the devil. Here, we are trapped inside the forms of birds and animals. They bring luck and the devil according to the priest's or the witches' words. Who sees you will determine what you are.

We are trapped in the painting. It speaks of God's work and the devil's; they run together like two feet. Yet as an onlooker I saw the figure of God outside looking down on it.

But the painter painted Him; it means He is in the painting, does it not?

The painter had to paint God into the creation.

Then God is in the painting just like us.

But God cannot be constrained by the painting like we are.

Who knows what God can do? It is us who created Him in our own image and likeness. God would never take on the human form, it is too dependent on another.

Another?

Man cannot exist without woman or woman without man. We must have both to procreate.

What are you saying?

God needs man to make Him all powerful.

You cannot say that God needs us.

Where would God be without us? We are in His image and likeness. Or He in ours.

We did not make God.

Yet we made Hell.

Because we are evil.

Then can we not make heaven because we are good? We can do what we want.

We cannot be who we want to be. I do not want to be a rabbit.

Nor me an owl.

Then why are we here?

This question has perplexed mankind since the beginning of time; surely you cannot expect me to answer it.

I meant, why are we in the painting?

Perhaps we are in another painting in the world outside. We may be creatures of paintings, not God. You will find out soon enough. The third panel calls you. You must move on.

Three is an unlucky number. It is death and hell that awaits. Besides, I am painted to the spot.

Yet you moved panels to get here. We must follow the path that destiny dictates because it is our own. Your destiny is in the next panel.

But that is in the depths of hell, worse than even the Inferno that Dante wrote about.

Perhaps we should think only that Dante believed enough in an After-life to write about it. He created his—your After-life awaits you now.

Hell? Then I will die.

Hell is that which we fear, to confront it is to tame it. Hell can only conquer us if we let it.

Brave words, but it is I that must seek out the truth of them.

Words, like paints, cannot hurt you; it is what lies within you that carries the demons. Seek out your fears then cast them out.

Magdalena wanted to shake her long floppy ears but she was frozen. *How can I reach it when I cannot even shake my ears?*

Think. Our thoughts transcend this world. The painting awaits you.

She wanted to respond but before she could she was in darkness. She was looking at the body of an upturned woman between her paws.

This dark world holds light. But how can a rabbit hold a woman? Her thoughts spilled out. They echoed from the heat and then answered.

Hell is our own making

Then I am damned and insane; my thoughts spill only to myself.

Our thoughts are always that, our own.

Then is hell my thought?

The acrid smell of smoke filled her nostrils as she looked at the lute and harp.

Can such beautiful instruments be played in hell?

She glanced up at the people happily eating inside the egg man.

Is hell what you make it?

Is life what you make it?

Is this world our creation, not God's?

Have we created boundaries of good and evil to mark our own path?

Magdalene closed her eyes then opened them. She was lying on the scullery floor. Had she dreamt the painting? It was impossible that she had entered into it, yet somehow she felt stronger. A rat ran across the floor; it was holding a strawberry that was too big for its mouth. When it saw her, it dropped it. The strawberry—the symbol of temptation—rolled along the floor. She picked it up and laughed.

SENTIENT PALATE
Sara Tantlinger

Quadruped creatures rustle through the low grass,
trying to taste those blue Atlas waters
and I am trying to taste
your flowery skin,
folding against me like a dancing organ.

Unspooled pleasure plants a garden of bursting cobalt,
reminding us to linger only among the bright berries
and the palate of light.
Do not journey into darkness where tongues cut you
    open,
do not allow yourself the taste of nightmares.

The scale mountain where corpses of dead fish
reinvent their rot into something almost sweet,
almost beautiful,
leads to another flesh orgy, desire without question,
bustles of orchids bloom from all your orifices,

and the strawberries spring to life, crawl through the
    low grass,
fuzzy, sentient fruit eating me,
or am I eating it?
All the tastes are scarlet nectar, juice or blood,
none of us can stop in the purgatory of constant
    enticement.

WITHIN THE GARDEN, RUNNING THROUGH

R. Bremner

*With thanks to Janet Kolstein
for her words, rearranged*

flash patina
bodies forms
melding insouciance
crooked crosses
sleek playground
swings around
shimmer marshland
conquer people
elephantine mystery
smile bight
tough enough
strangers factory
perfumed ambition
rapid change
invaders gilded
fleshy crumbs
oily hustings
anonymous hands
swish and sway
in historic ripe
beyond arithmetic

PARADISUM VOLUPTATIS
Joanna Koch

I

Nate and I stagger out into the sunlight on Colfax. The plateau of concrete and Denver's altitude intensify the glare. I cover my eyes and Nate shields his groin as though the sensory assault is directed between his legs. Of course neither of us have sunglasses.

"Jesus, I'm blind," I tell Nate's hand.

He turns to my voice with a slurred half-smile, acknowledging the sound. I don't expect a response. Nate likes my voice. He never listens to what I say. That's why I'm so into him.

I'm not the type to cheat on my boyfriend and get drunk by two p.m. on a Wednesday. Or any day. Nate and I share some unspoken agreement that the rules don't apply with us. It happened the first time we met. I hated myself, but I needed the magic. Nate probably needed a doctor. Not that I cared. So we keep meeting. Instead of studying for class or cello practice, I curse Denver's pristine sky and try not to face-plant on the sidewalk.

"We need some pot," Nate says. Then he laughs. I don't know what the joke is. "I know a guy on Zuni."

I say, "Man, I used to live on Zuni. They've got pig faces in the grocery store up there."

"Yeah, I know," Nate says. "Come on."

It's a long way to Zuni, so we stop for a fifth or a pint or whatever it is. I can never remember. Nate knows exactly what to say. The guy behind the counter at the liquor store looks Nate up and down and then looks at me like I'm for sale. Nate's a regular. He's there every day. When we leave, Nate says he's going to tell the guy I'm his daughter. "And then next time we go in, we'll make out in front of him. Can you imagine?"

I don't want you to think I'm a bad person. Eric, loosely defined as my boyfriend, views me as an accessory. I'm just part of the outfit he wears for public events when he comes home tired after weeks away on assignment. Affection is out of the question. Sex is hit and run. When I try to talk about our problem, my thoughts deconstruct as they fall out of my mouth. Eric micro-analyzes every word into oblivion. Talking twists it all into my fault, my failings, my lack of experience and unreasonable demands. I offer to leave. He begs me to stay. Eric's made a million promises and then chastised me for speaking up when he didn't keep them. He's used my voice as a weapon against me.

Nate's never listened, never worked, and never promised me shit. Alcohol unites us. Nothing is real, everything is permitted. When intoxication curbs Nate's agility, we get creative. "God, you're nasty," Nate whispers with awe. It doesn't feel like cheating. It feels like a vacation in Interzone.

"Baby, this is so cool," Nate says. Beyond downtown, the rocky path along the viaduct is un-gentrified. Gang tags, shoes without mates and rotting toys mark the trail. A path of broken glass breadcrumbs glitter in the dirt, leading stray children to or from the witch's house: who cares what direction? A path is a path. Nate's always on his way to find something.

A block before Zuni, a white bag blows out of the bushes like a little ghost rising to greet us. It crackles end over end along the gutter to snatch at our feet. The faces behind the dim windows of a cheap retirement home glow, watching us without seeing. They line up like puffballs in a fairy ring unstrung to conform to a linear narrative, forced out of their circle to concede to time. They look the same now as five years ago when I first came to Denver. Featureless from age, pale sentries grow atop stalks rooted in a lifeless medium. I stop. The baby ghost bag yields to us. Nate banishes it with the tip of his black Chelsea boot and pulls me onward.

"See that?" he says. "When you're drunk long enough it's like you're on acid. Then when you get stoned it's like, you know... this is going to be great. We've been drunk for what, two days?"

"I'm not drunk," I say. We almost trip over each other laughing.

The guy on Zuni is gone, back to Juarez. Nate talks his way into the house anyway.

"Our shit is better than weed," the new guy says when Nate gets around to asking. I've never bought drugs. I didn't know you had to socialize. The vodka is gone and the house smells like boiling baloney. Damp, too. The men trickling from room to room don't look at me like I'm for sale. They look at me like I'm lunch.

"How much?" Nate asks.

The guy hands him a little Hello Kitty pillbox filled with colorless gunk that looks like lip balm. "Two fifty."

"You're killing me."

"Two twenty-five. Last forever, bruh."

"Serious."

"Two-ten, last chance. Try it out."

"How?"

"Rub it on your ear, wherever. Your lady gonna freak, see."

Nate puts a dab on his finger, rubs his ear, and holds the gunk out to me. I shake my head. Nate puts his pinky in the gunk and says, "Come on, baby. I want you to get stoned with me." He brushes the back of his hand across my cheek. At moments like this, Nate is almost loving, almost tender. Nate's finger slides into my ear and I taste oak in the back of my mouth, like the finish on a fine red.

I feel the oak in my teeth. Music comes out of them. The men's voices slow down and grow deep like the undulating bass line of a soul song. High, windy tones splash through the open window. It's traffic, urging me to accede.

The pores in my skin exalt as if each one has an independent breath. They hyperventilate, an echoing chorus high on oxygen. The sound of Nate's screaming slices through the music. He's unbuttoned my shirt and then fallen back in panic. The other men shush him. I see they wear masks. I follow their stares to my chest and seek my reflection in the black screen of a dead television. In place of my breasts, a symmetrical set of enormous ears opens like the wings of a butterfly.

My voice silences Nate's squeal. My voice grinds like the tires on the asphalt outside from a whisper to a roar. Then all is quiet. A man with a shit-eating grin approaches me and says, "Check this out." He sinks to his knees and blows across my chest. The ears tingle. I gasp.

His mask covers only the top right quadrant of his face. His tongue protrudes like a reptile. He flicks his tongue across my left lobe and exhales into the aural canal. Fine cilia play a symphony within. He circles, breathing deliberately and barely touching the ear until the music melts into liquid and spills out. His head swerves and he sinks his teeth into the lobe.

His neck is exposed. Heats cut through the center of my chest. A knife springs forth between the ears and slashes his dirty throat, dousing my torso in his blood, warm and wet.

"Holy fuck," Nate says.

The other men gibber and scurry. I grab the Hello Kitty pillbox Nate's dropped. I smear the gunk across the flat edge of the knife and enjoy the blade quivering in ecstatic response. This is what an erection feels like, I guess. I pull the knife from between the ears on my chest and sink it into my right eye. Colors explode. Many-faceted insects fly like diamonds from my eye in an army of knives that plunge into the fleeing and fortifying men. My eye sits on the tip of every blade, buried in their hearts, their lungs, their guts. My eyes stay alive inside them for centuries, watching them rot. Their bodies feed roots reaching into the future and the past, roots of the fungal mind-web living inside the earth.

Half-blind, I recognize the pox behind their masks. She came from the stars eons ago and inoculated our unborn planet. Creation spread like a contagion, a disease breeding many imposters and known by many names. Before the sixteenth century, physicians agreed all illness sprang from a single source. The pedigree of infection traced the disease of life to one fertile spore. Miasma poisoned the air, effluvium spread her symptoms. She was afforded proper worship until she bared her naked face at the close of the fourteenth century. Syphilis masqueraded through medieval Europe, and one hundred years of case histories quantified the Divine Pox: the smallest minds of the millennium replaced a deity with a diagnosis.

Her ancient roots grow through my multitude of eyes and the dead men on the ground and the wet floor of the house on Zuni Street. Where Nate cowers, a white oak spawns multiple trunks that erupt like sudden mushrooms in the damp house. Their gnarled arms communicate simultaneous narratives interlocking through hidden tree rings. History and the future connect within them like a chain linked from end to end in a circle. The clasp holds the chain together inside our warm flesh as a warning bell peals into the present day from fifteenth century Europe: once we map the New World, Eden is impossible.

Before 1490, the fungal arms of white oak

bloomed on all corners of the planet from shared roots like mad, insistent corals. Her trunks were felled, planed, and sized, made ready to receive the pigment and prayer of craftsmen and artists. Layers of animal skin glue and gesso failed to obscure the living message carried in her veins. Medieval altarpieces hewn of her provenance intoxicated congregations by their mere presence. As time aged and desiccated the panels, curators harvested her sap as a sacramental balm, further depleting her potency. In the modern age, only the boldest heresy retains a trace.

The silence of the Inquisition on this matter proves their complicity with the argument embedded in the wood: a tree grows within a forest underneath the ground, an ancient fungal infection, a mind that mutates men into fruiting bodies of her will. "You are liars or fools who say I traveled to the Old World on the ships of Columbus or Cortez. I am endemic wherever there is life. Man is my vessel, and through him I will repopulate the stars. I am in the earth, but I am not of the earth."

"Baby," Nate says, scuffling through the carnage. "Babe, I can't understand you but I think we have to go."

Nate's voice again is gentle, tender, almost loving. But I don't need him to understand. I need him to hear. I need him to hurt me. I need him to hurt. I need him to come with me and stumble onto the sidewalk or into the abyss or out of this allegory and throw wide open the flat panels pinning us like a forgotten butterfly collection to the surface of things. I need him to help me come out from behind the glass.

"As above, so below," I decree. Nate pauses in his rush to escape the chaos. He peers at me in his shy way with his slurred smile. He's always been shy, started drinking young to manage his anxiety. Kept drinking to drown his father's voice calling him a fag because he liked art and fixed his sister's hair. Nate wanted to make his world more beautiful and ended up making it a slum. I met him when his life was done, when his stories were over-told and his clever ideas recycled, when his daughter refused to see him again and his ex-wives milked him dry. When I met him, Nate had nothing to offer me. I took it.

Nate holds my wrist and dips his finger in the little tub of gunk. He paints it onto my upper lip, dips again, and works on the lower with careful strokes until he's satisfied with the effect. His grip around my wrist leaves the watermark of his fingertips in my skin. His shy glance asks me if I recognize him: the hero playing the vagabond. I try to remain inscrutable. He kisses me. We drink the melting substance smashed between our lips with the seven tongues of a dragon he's slain and kept hidden in his pocket.

We lap up the gunk. I unzip his jeans and sheath him in the stuff. New parts spring forth in all directions. The receptive ones I plumb, spreading the substance and expanding organs that bloom between us like meaty flowers. I mount him, roots form, and the dead men around us stir. Nate's chasm widens. We plunge inside and eat the fruit.

In the New World, we find many strange and wondrous creatures. Birds of every color fly through air and water; rhinoceros, lion, and unicorn roam free upon the land. Men live like beasts, prized for their animal beauty and strength. Women suckle their young, unashamed. Exotic specimens both human and animal are brought to the auction block and deemed free of blemish by my European ancestors who trade their civilized microbial gifts of smallpox, measles, and typhus in exchange for the New World's abundant crops. Mercenaries are imported, slaves are sold, Eden is exploited.

The great explorers, masters of navigating by the stars, surveyed their course according to the trajectory of reason. Those who donned the mask of syphilis in their old age deemed it the worthy price of enlightenment. Certainly, the stars would not lie.

    I fuck Nate's voluptuous new orifice. It fucks me, and grips me, and sucks me dry. I see my face reflected in Nate's obsidian skin, doubled by the twin globes of his ass. The eyes that look back at me are feral and empty, diseased by a Tudor kiss.

II

"You're home early."

I creep under the covers. It's three in the morning. "I didn't think you'd be here today."

"Yesterday."

"Sorry." I press into Eric, feeling his disgust.

Eric shifts, turns over, makes a barricade of sheets between our bodies. "We wrapped early. Extra pay." Eric makes military training films. It's not the creative work he craves, but it pays the bills. I've told him to quit. He's a painter by vocation. His brushes, paints, and rolls of canvas clutter the back of the closet. Paint tubes harden. Brushes lose their hair. Eric says we can't waste money on studio space. I say use the living room. He says that's irresponsible, what would people think. I say who cares, you have to live and that's what it's for. He says well, we can't all just do what we want, can we? I say why not? At some point in the rhetorical mess, Eric goes deaf.

I destroy all chance of an alibi. I don't want one. "You got back yesterday last night or yesterday Monday?"

Eric sighs. "Today is Thursday."

"Oh. Right." I sit up and look at Eric in the red glow of ambient light from the twenty-four hour diner across the street. "What have you been doing for two days? Why didn't you call?"

Eric doesn't move. His body is an inscrutable landscape in the near dark, his voice an empty echo. "What have I been doing. Why didn't I call. Are you prepared to have a serious conversation at this hour?"

"No. I mean, I'm not prepared, I'm just, you know, concerned. I'm sorry. What did you do all this time?"

"Looked for you."

"I'm sorry."

"Stop saying that."

"But I am. Why didn't you call?"

"Go to sleep."

Inside me, there's a cathedral in flames. Ergot dancers surround the spires, casting obscene shadows in the red-tinged light as an apocalypse cracks the sky open like a raw egg. The man beside me doesn't see the figures licking the walls or the glare on the ceiling. He doesn't acknowledge the dizzying altitude of young mountains aglow with black and red wildfire that eats the trees. He's impervious to their screams. He doesn't ask me where I've been.

Tonight I told Nate it was over. Again. It wasn't the first time and it won't be the last. I'd tell Eric the same if he'd hear me. I'm sick of being the middle panel of our triptych, an incomplete story if I lose either wing. I can't survive as a solitary point in history, a grey globe interred by redundant chastity, closed and colorless, endlessly enduring the inertia of time's static symmetry. I need to fall off the flat edge of the world and embrace our collective fate. I want to fall: fall into the pit, or fly into the clouds, or both. If Hell is a product of history, Eden is a relic of eternity. Opposites conjugate in a compositional destination that binds the three of us together. We're hinged by the navigational rivalry of derelict stars. When we open our wings to take flight, we reverse the Fall of Man. If the end result is a fantasy or a satire, at least we'll sabotage the sequential face of history as we sail into the fire.

Eric's body is a warm, rhythmic beast beside me. Asleep, there's no anger on his face, no suspicion or disdain. He walks in the garden, the paradise that never existed outside an older man's dream of Eve's fidelity. He ignores the swans with too many heads, the restless gaze of owls. I slough off Eric's cocoon of sheets, exposing his flesh to my fingers. He's muscular, but his surface has softened with age into something both firm and pliant. I caress the paradox of his back. He's mistaken about Eve. She's not demure. She cuts across antiquity to expose the Father of Man as an imposter. Eve doesn't look down out of modesty or fear. She looks down out of boredom and resignation. Adam isn't enough.

When Eve looks up, and always she must, the future rages like a newborn pestilence. Enlightenment ravages the populace. Time spirals outward. Eric breathes less deeply as I draw my hands across his skin. I reach between his strong legs and brush the head of his lust as it bucks. Something involuntary and joyful like this grows inside me too. Maybe this time we'll evolve. Maybe this time we'll make it work. I want Eric to have more than one head, more than one life, more than one chance for enlightenment. One life is not enough. I wake him by pressing him into me where I'm still wet. His eyes stay closed. I'm careful to keep silent.

We fit together too well. Our incongruities shock. We came west together seeking emotional gold. The new delighted us. At the Mercado on Zuni, we practiced our Spanish with lavishly rolled *R*s until I halted at the deli case. Pig heads lined up before me with eyeless sockets. They stared like the heads in the window of the retirement home, watching without seeing, like unstrung puffballs in a fairy ring forced out of their circle to concede to linear time. Reflected in the deli glass, my face was transposed with the face of a dead pig.

The glare of sunlight obliterated the image. "Be careful," Eric said. "You'll hurt your eyes." He touched my back. I jumped. Purple sunspots skewed my smile into a grimace.

Eric pulled back. He's been orbiting away ever since. The harder I reach for him, the further away he recedes. We make love rarely, without speaking or looking. In public we're the portrait of a happy couple, but beneath our painted surface, the mute flesh of butchered animals holds a primal grudge. Our muscles remember every cut, our severed flesh sags, and our gouged eyes are blind. We wear masks of deception. We live behind glass.

We live until we die or mutate. Fungal hyphae network through both the soil below and the spatio-temporal heavens above. My body is an arm of the organism, inoculating Eric with spores of the disease that will transform us into a unified, animated host. We are destined for space exploration in the New World. We are bound for undying love. We are bound to Nate and the dead men on Zuni and the thinking underground forest that entangles us in her divine web. She rewards us with her sticky glory.

As we enter and exit one another, advancing and retreating, coupling and uncoupling, Eric grows louder, almost looking, almost shouting. I haven't heard him like this in ages, haven't felt him take me like this in so long that I forget all motivation apart from my body and its construct of lust. I feed him its sacrament. I'm not sure about the consequences or the price. I'm sure that at this moment we're in a place more holy than any terrestrial church. Take, eat, this is my body.

But what if my body eats him first?

III

I'm drinking a complicated red with a smooth finish, tasting oak in the back of my throat. The syphilis bacterium is shaped like a corkscrew. The irony isn't lost on me. I wear the life-token of the many-named plague in the scars on my chest. With age, my body has become a symphony of scars. Textures, creases, enlarging follicles, sunspots, and tan lines blur into swarthy meat. My skin sings of illness. The drinks don't blur things like they used to, but I'll let you buy them if you like. I'm waiting for a friend.

I drove from Wisconsin to Denver without a reservation last night. Some insane chemical GPS called me to the Mercury Club like the rest of this throng. It's been ten years. Everyone looks like they came here to meet a blind date, eyeing one another, wondering when the show starts. I guess I'm not the only one who felt the call. Perhaps you felt it too.

It's getting late and you, my new found friend, have listened to my story of love exploited and lost. I hope you don't think less of me. A triptych is a trap. In traditional form, the imaginary timelines of theology and the confluence of themes bind each panel to the rest. As separate entities, significance is lost, context is infinite. Randomly cropped remnants persist as puzzles the future may never unlock. What happens between creation and apocalypse? Is the middle panel the subject or the object? What sensation survives between lovers when we reject the boredom of the story and its conveyance? A triptych is engineered to be stable and portable. You carry it on your back when it's closed. It's almost a funny thought: an altarpiece like a traveling salesman's display ready to be propped up and gawked at.

"You're a woman of mystery," you say.

I roll my eyes. "You don't know me."

"I've seen you play."

"A triptych enfolds the viewer the way I hold my

cello, like a lover between my legs, like a mother giving birth to an ekphrasis. She's an instrument from the Age of Reason, a Renaissance girl. You think she's austere, but deep down she's as needy as the rest of us. She begs to be plucked and bowed and strummed."

You say, "Mother, I want the sun."

"Excuse me?"

"Ghosts. I'm also on the stage, in theater. I'm Oswald."

I ask, "Is this research for your role?"

You answer, "It's more than that. My role makes me wonder what the world might be without the burden of a dead patriarch on its back."

"It's like you can read my mind. How many father figures do I have to destroy to escape this allegory? I have a thing for artists, especially the ones who don't make any art. Why is that so common? Why do so many great men fear genius and fall prey to the mundane? Don't you agree that the sexual and aesthetic goal of life is unencumbered freedom?"

You start to speak with a soft inhalation, and then interrupt your own breath when an old man and his caregiver enter the club. Your body moves like an act of grace, vanishing to an adjacent table.

I recognize Nate right away. He ducks through the doorway. His wavering frame in a vintage blazer hasn't changed. Same precarious height and poor connection, like his head will float away from his feet any second in a cloud of cigarette smoke. An older white guy accompanies Nate. He's shorter, disabled, and it's not until he leans over to peck my cheek that I realize he's not older, he's Eric. His body smells like sulfur.

Eric acclimates to the seat on my right side, his body unbending at the joints. Nate lilts into the seat on my left like liquid.

Nate's half-smile half-glance half-love expression molds his face into a permanent caricature of himself. Or maybe he's drunk. Of course he's drunk. Eric is stone sober and won't let up on the eye contact, the demanding veracity of his vision. He's an artist with no model, a painter with no canvas, a starving hawk. His eyes accuse me and excuse me from above. I'm not a person to him. I'm prey. I take his hand, and Nate's.

"I can't believe you're here. I didn't know you two... um," I say.

"Yeah," Nate offers. "Well, someone had to take care of him."

The violence in Eric's eyes belies his gentle tone of voice. "After you left, he kept coming by. I don't pretend to know what you do. I have always been supportive. As you can see, I needed assistance."

Nate does that thing where he makes a kissy noise sucking on his cigarette. I want to kick him every time he smokes a cigarette. He says, "Don't blame her, dude."

Eric's face looks like bitten fruit. His flesh is puckered and rotten. "This isn't easy for me. I'm not here to blame anyone. You didn't have to hide anything from me."

Nate says, "She was young."

Eric says, "You didn't have to lie. Why did you lie?"

Their hands feel like two different species. Nate's thin fingers seep away from my grip. He's got a drink and a cigarette to tend. Eric clasps my fret hand like a threat. I pull it away out of instinct. It's been my livelihood all these years.

Eric says, "You didn't tell me you were sick."

"I wasn't."

Eric doesn't hear me. Nate says, "It's my fault."

"I'm not talking to you," Eric snaps at Nate and then turns back to me. His hand is still open, expectant. "I will always care about you."

Parallel conversations ebb and flow around the club with similar hushed intensity. Each table flickers, candle at the center, black and red décor absorbing ambient light. Faces in various stages of decay implore, debate, and confess, a gallery of grotesque, unthinkable masks poised for a ceremony to start. You, my friend, my spy, solitary and silhouetted by the glow of your phone, wait attentively as the human narrative exhausts itself.

Eric's premise is all wrong. I speak to you as much as to him. "Do you want me to be a bird with its wings sliced off, a shark with its fins amputated for soup, sinking to the depths and dying of immobility?"

"Don't be sad," Nate says.

"Stay out of this," Eric says to Nate, and then to me: "I'm trying to forgive you."

Nate says, "Nothing to forgive. I'm making amends."

Eric's eyes flash. "Is that what you call it? Free rent and free food, probably peddling my meds. I should throw you back on the street."

"Don't talk to him like that," I say to Eric.

"Hey, hey, it's okay," Nate says. "I mean, it is what it is. Somebody's got to take care of him. I got this, baby." Nate's body flows in close to me while Eric's rigid posture of pain nails him upright in his seat.

"This is all very touching," Eric says from a distance. "Don't you feel any remorse?"

I'm not sure which one of us he's talking to but I'm ready to answer. "Time wasn't supposed to be so fucking linear. It was a gift. Something we shared. I saw us growing and moving together and burning what we left behind."

"That's why you poisoned me? As a gift?" Eric's voice isn't so gentle anymore. Heads turn.

"It's not poison. Look around you."

"I'm dying," Eric says.

Nate says, "The forest is dying."

Roots below and above are withered. Hyphae

joining us through the fungal network burn away in the glare of modernity. Called by the chemical signals of an ancient organism's death-throes, we're a poorly reconstructed triptych, an anachronism. Looking around this somber congregation, I can barely imagine these beings as the frolicking, fruiting bodies of our shared, toxic vision; pale, inverted and many-limbed; joyful, innocent and wanton as we combine into a heretical geometry, a blueprint of paradox, an illuminated neuro-script. Our bodies will reconfigure into a manic vessel, the spaceship *Paradisum Voluptatis*. She will carry us aloft into the New World.

I say, "When we leave, this will be a dead planet. We're gathered for lift-off."

"This is fun," Nate says.

"This is bullshit," says Eric. "Let's go."

Nate's eyes almost open all the way. Eric fights to extract himself from his chair. His face reddens with effort. "She's crazier than ever. This is pointless. Do you understand?" Eric turns to me. "You know you need help. There's a cure. Sometimes it works." He struggles against the confines of his body. I can infer from his movements the ineffable beauty of the multi-dimensional, asymmetrical being Eric refuses to become.

I make one last attempt to reach him. "The cure is killing you."

Standing, leaning, Eric catches his breath and shakes his head. "Bat-shit crazy bullshit." He hobbles away, relying on his cane.

"Babe, I gotta motor." Nate's up and ready to follow. He's about a foot taller than me. He gets in so close I have to look up to see him. He says, "Call me. Okay?"

"What do you mean? If you stay, you'll die like him."

"Aw, I knew you loved me best. I won't tell. Almost forgot. I brought you something." Nate hands me a plastic baggy with some tablets of various shapes inside. Lint from his pocket is stuck to the baggy and the plastic is crumpled from re-use. It's no longer transparent.

Nate crushes me into his chest, leans down and puts his lips in my hair. "You loved me best."

"I—"

He says, "Shh."

I loved the idea of the man more than the man himself. I've looked for him, mourned for him, and known him by the singing of my scars, by the seven tongues hidden in his filthy pocket. He leaves one of them with me, bitten and dry. He leaves.

My spy, my snake, my newest friend, you palm the baggy and take the seat across from me. You're welcome to take them both. You say: "The faces we wear in this world are masks." You have effete cheekbones and glorious skin, and eyes still clear and bright with the ignorant kindness of youth. I suspect you've led a privileged life. You speak in a way that is wise, yet you can't possibly know that I avoid mirrors lest I see in my reflection the face of a dead pig.

I answer you as honestly as I can. "Beneath our feet, god is dying. The disease of life demands the stars."

"Does it? You share some colloquy?" You shift your shoulders forward and say "colloquy" as if I know what the word means. Your eyes are full of light and aspiration. "Will you share with me?" you ask.

Old sources of the sacrament have dried up. The antibiotics of the twentieth century eradicated most of our kind, and collectors of medieval art no longer guard the sacred argument of the hallucinatory sap. The drug is legendary, and outside of our bodies, it is lost, lost. My radiant new friend, the world is ripe for a new plague, and you're burning with faith. Who am I to stop time in her tracks? Why, indeed, would the stars ever lie?

You are naked and gleam like quicksilver, as though impervious to time. I'm less naked than you, but no less monstrous standing on the frontier of disintegration. I know Creation is a plague. I know that when desire transforms into violence, I will participate in the drama.

"Aren't you a bit young for this scene?"

"That's not important," you lie to me. "You're beautiful."

"I don't know if you're ready for this. Maybe you should take some of those pills."

"I don't need that," you say.

"Are you sure?"

The congregation's culled to less than fifty. Outside, we assemble into forms indeterminate as animal or vegetable or rock. We enact pornographic tableau, an exploded model of a medieval simultaneous stage. The chain of time closes and locks. Mycelia weave our raw nerves as one tendril, pulsating with ancient and modern thought. In the city, polluted by artificial light, the stars have gone blind. Orifices able to give and receive chart a didactic course as they increase. We navigate by multiplicity. The *Paradisum Voluptatis* ascends to the night sky with the glory of a symphony, an armed battalion greater than the sum of her parts.

Your heart beats too fast, your muscles clench. I told you to take the pills. I turn you over and push your face into the earth, our foster mother. You spit in her dirt and murmur your lines, "The sun, the sun." I pull back from the warm knot of your colon and release its new trickle of blood. To soothe you, I whisper in your ear as you grow limbs, voices, eyes:

"I'm the flat color on oak, the pigment cracked by age. What harm can I do to you? My waters are pictures of water. My lust is a satire of lust. My church is a creature inside you, a spore that spreads when you dream. My church is a doctrine of deception, a mask of love and horror. You wear it when you dream. Your dream is a weapon of desire; your body is the fruit of my dreams. Your body is the fruit of syphilis."

I press you into a new shape. We rise.

III

THE LAST
LAST CHANCE
PARADE

WHY DO BIRDS SUDDENLY APPEAR?
Rajiv Moté

The curious gathered in the courtyard to watch the pale, naked man shuffle towards the light spilling through the black arch. His limbs were bone, wasted muscle, and sagging skin, hanging like sticks from his bloated torso. He had no hair. Some of the watchers made to cover their own nakedness with their hands, or twist their bodies from the light in sympathetic shame, but none looked away. The light cut through the inky shadows, not angry and red like the distant volcanic fire, but brilliant and golden. Against it, the man's skin looked translucent as fog. From beyond the gatehouse came sounds that could be heard nowhere else in Hell. Laughter. Song. To the watchers, the light and merriment on the other side of the arch felt nothing less than holy.

"Do you think they'll let him pass, Jaan?"

Everyone lingered in the courtyard, despite the danger, wondering the same. The irresistible drama of redemption, if that was what this was, gave meaning to this world of suffering. They spoke in whispers and watched the man's progress, their eyes flickering to the sky, ready to scatter if their loitering was noticed.

"We'll see, Tessa."

Repeating each other's names was a ritual between them. It was also, in its own way, holy. They couldn't remember if those were their true names, but they clung to them. The names stirred something just shy of a memory, a feeling of being together, enclosed, safe. From the corner of his eye, Jaan tried to memorize details of Tessa's face—the red-gold hair, high forehead, blue eyes, lobeless ears, thin lips, sharply tapered chin—but as his eyes moved over each feature he forgot the previous. Memory was slippery, and fragile as thin glass. Once, he thought, that her face meant something to him. If he could just hold its parts together in his mind, he might remember what.

The man's feet dragged on the gray stone of the courtyard, never lifting enough to break contact. It took him time.

"Ought he approach penitent or proud, Tessa?"

"I can't remember, Jaan."

Before the arch was the Gatekeeper, tall and sinister in his feathered cloak and tufted helm. He allowed some of those who approached to pass. Others, he punished horrifically, their remains strewn across the courtyard to crawl and knit themselves together. Jaan remembered that, but trying to discern a pattern was like grasping at smoke.

The man stopped his shuffling and stood in front of the Gatekeeper, his gaze downcast. The Gatekeeper regarded him with eyes that shone round and yellow beneath the helm. He circled the man slowly, occasionally grasping at a body part with a claw-like hand, as though judging the ripeness of fruit. Jaan felt a flush of shame, and nearly averted his eyes. Bodies were so shameful.

Tessa's hand reached and clasped Jaan's, and he looked down at the sudden, unexpected contact. Touch without pain unnerved him. His eyes crept up her arm to her shoulder, and rested on her breasts, hanging like fleshy pears above her ribs. Then his gaze sank lower to the red-gold thatch of hair where her pale legs met. They once meant something to him, those parts of her. Tessa's hand withdrew, and she tried to cover herself.

"No, Jaan. Don't look."

He became aware of his own nakedness, and recoiled. He had a ghost of a memory of the sickly-sweet taste of fruit, a lifting veil, and the slow billowing of bone-deep shame. The shame was an unclean itch marbled deep into his flesh, and when it flared, he craved the deliverance of scouring punishment.

"I'm sorry, Tessa."

They returned their eyes to the man, being prodded and inspected by the Gatekeeper. Jaan's fists clenched and his nails drew blood. From the corner of his eye, he spied revulsion on Tessa's face.

The Gatekeeper continued circling and groping the man who stood motionless before him. Jaan stepped back, anticipating a spray of blood. But the Gatekeeper stopped, and with a mocking bow, motioned the man under the arch. He shuffled forward, hastened by a hard smack across his buttocks, and disappeared into the golden light.

A commotion of talk exploded in the courtyard.

"He was accepted!"

"Did anybody know him?"

"He expiated all his sin!"

"How did he do it?"

"Should I try?"

Neither proud nor penitent, Jaan thought. The man came... empty. Motion caught Jaan's eye. He looked up.

"Birds!" cried someone.

All eyes drew skyward. The black, jumbled shapes of wings, beaks, and talons burst through the sooty clouds in utter silence. There were birds and there were Birds, and these were the latter. Insufficiently tormented souls eventually drew Birds. They were living voids, bird-shaped holes in the universe, and they inspired primeval horror beyond all torture when they appeared. Suffering had purpose, the only purpose: atonement. So it was believed. But the Birds were nothing, an absence, a horror of meaninglessness, the annihilation of all possibility. Facing them was beyond anyone's courage. The people in the courtyard scattered.

"Jaan!"

"Tessa!"

They ran. Flagstone became jagged rock that tore at the soles of their feet, but the pain was not enough. They ran faster. A hanging tree twisted up near the road, its branches already heavy with dangling figures kicking their legs and wheezing against the rope around their throats. Birds of a more ordinary sort pecked at their flesh, tearing off gobbets. It was good, honest torture. Irreproachable. But there were no unoccupied nooses. Tessa moaned. Jaan could not bring himself to glance at the sky. They ran on.

On the hills above their path, the citadel burned. It always burned. Figures fetched buckets from the lake and scrambled up ladders, trying to quench the blaze as more fires sprung up for each they put out. They, and the citadel's defenders, plummeted from the walls, succumbing to flames, or the arrows and spears from the Fell Hordes below. The endless war was unwinnable, but the souls on the ramparts were grateful to fight it. From the time he spent there, Jaan knew it was an exquisite torture of perpetual despair and defeat. But he and Tessa could never make it to the walls before the Birds were upon them. So they kept running, towards the hopeful sounds of rushing water and screaming. A bridge emerged from the darkness, and soon Jaan saw the river. Pale, bloated bodies floated in the current, dying but not dead, never dead.

Jaan smiled. He seized Tessa's red-brown hair and balled his fist. "Tessa," he said.

"Jaan," she answered.

He smashed his fist into her nose. She crumpled, her blue eyes filled with gratitude, and tumbled over the low railing. The hairs on his neck stiffened. He sensed silence descending on him like a crushing mass. He froze in panic, his mind screaming to throw himself into the river, and his body refusing to obey.

Suddenly, excruciating pain pierced his heart, and Jaan looked down to see the tip of a lance emerge from his chest. He twisted his neck to see the Horned King behind him, astride his rat. His Fell Hordes of clawed, fanged, spiked monsters bristled with weapons behind him, on their way to the citadel. With relief, Jaan submitted to the agony as the Horned King raised his lance and Jaan slid along its length. The King then lowered his lance with a twist, and Jaan slipped down the blood-slick wood and tumbled into the river of bodies.

***

Jaan floated. His body bobbed with the current and caromed off other bodies. The water, growing colder the further it swept him, flooded his nose and mouth as the swells filled the troughs. It bubbled up through the hole in his chest, injecting agony into his heart's attempt to heal. He drowned and froze and bled and embraced the pain, knowing at last he was safe from the Birds.

"Tessa," he said. But he lost grasp of what the word meant.

Having found a steady source of pain at last, Jaan could let go. Relieved of fear of Birds, and the anxiety of an existence without progress or purpose, he could devote himself to his atonement, to burning away the shame that infested him to his marrow. Securely in torment, he even amused himself with idle thoughts, like pondering the origin of shame. Once, a long while ago, or perhaps recently—time had no meaning—he'd asked the Owl, for the Owl was ancient and wise, and had gifted him with unimaginable pain.

"There was once a thing called sin," the Owl said, before carefully slicing open the flesh at Jaan's heel with a talon. "Sin is a bloody, sticky rawness in men that adheres to the world and separates them from their Maker. An abhorrent, repulsive condition. Shame is your awareness of sin. Your knowledge of its wrongness. Is it not terrible?"

Jaan frowned through the pain blossoming in his foot. Memory was slippery, but he knew there was a moment, something with a sickly-sweet taste, when he learned shame. If such a moment existed, there must have been moments before he knew shame. Before there was sin. He put this to the Owl.

The great bird hooted, an amused sound. "So, a philosopher!" The Owl delicately peeled the skin from Jaan's heel in a single narrow strip around his foot, tracing between his toes and spiraling slowly up his leg. "Your Maker began you, but you are not yet complete. Finishing yourselves is your purpose." Pain blazed through Jaan. Not just where the flesh was removed, but everywhere.

"You were meant to eat of the fruit. You were meant to open your eyes. Shame is a teacher. Heed it, and let it guide you."

Jaan remembered hearing the Owl's calm words despite his screams. He was hung by his hands, bound to a great harp by its strings, and while the Owl peeled, his struggles strummed a gentle counterpoint to his raw-throated cries. In some walled-off corner of Jaan's mind, he heard a tiny whisper: *Tessa*.

"Suffering roasts away the rawness and attachment. It makes you perfect. Pleasing to your Maker."

His Maker. There was something forbidden by his Maker, something that brought him a sense of purpose and incomprehensible shame, all at once.

The Owl was a master craftsman. Before it regrew, Jaan's entire rind, a glistening red ribbon looping on the ground, was uniform and unbroken, beautiful in its perfection.

***

"Tessa." He spoke the name, and icy water filled his mouth, making him sputter. There once was a face that meant something. Blue eyes. Red hair. Or was it gold? The tiny part of him tucked away from the agony, the part he thought of as himself, grasped at the pieces, trying to fit them together as they sliced his fingers, a puzzle of shattered glass. He floated, froze, drowned, and collided with other bodies. He floated forever, or a short while. Time had no meaning.

"Tessa," he said.

"Jaan," he heard.

Jaan raised his head, upsetting the equilibrium that kept him afloat. His limbs thrashed, and razor shards of ice sliced his skin. And he saw her, a few bodies downstream, a rime of frost covering the parts of her above the water. Jaan crawled over the bodies, sending them into choking, gasping fits. His hand reached out, and found hers. They clasped. Again came that uneasy feeling of contact, with neither pain nor shame. A raised whip that never fell. So cold, and yet... Her. *Tessa*. The tiny oasis from the agony that was himself shyly touched the tucked-away part of her that whispered his name. And they adhered, merged, making a shared, hidden space, a crystalline bubble containing only themselves.

Jaan. The name flowed through their connection.

Tessa. The name flowed back. The names echoed in the bubble, sustaining themselves.

Time had no meaning.

Jaan learned that misery and its absence don't exclude one another. They're adjacent countries with artificial borders, and sometimes one can choose where to stand, where to live. Creatures under the water took bites of their flesh, shards of ice cut them, the water itself continued to freeze and drown them. Jaan suffered, he wept, and at times he screamed. As did Tessa. But that was the way of things, the rules. What one did. It was not what they *were*. Their hidden selves, Jaan and Tessa, lay entwined in their bubble, separate from what Hell demanded of them.

Hand in hand they floated, souls joined, straddling the boundary between agony and secret joy. Enough agony to avoid Birds, enough joy to nurture the space they shared. Arrows from the Fell Hordes on the banks struck them, the monsters that hid deep in the water rose and feasted on their flesh, and ice floes sliced them to ribbons. But they always found each other again. They drew each other in as surely as the arch and courtyard drew those hopeful for salvation. It could all be endured.

"Could we stay like this, Tessa? Forever balancing?"

"What is forever, Jaan? This is how we are. Until something changes."

"Nothing ever changes, Tessa."

"Then yes, Jaan. For now, we can be like this forever."

Their bubble grew. By increments they shaped it into a garden of sunlight, blue skies, green trees, fruits, flowers, and life. It was memory, not fanciful invention. Memory could be rediscovered in this space. Here, memories stayed. They remembered a world before Hell, where joy was unadulterated and shame, absent. They remembered taking pleasure in their bodies, and each other's. There was no sin there. They must have been taught their shame. They sported in sun-warmed pools, ate fruit and the flesh of fair beasts, and danced in the hills and forests. Jaan found the sweetness of the memory so intense, it was almost its own torture. He couldn't remember feeling so keenly in the garden.

"We didn't know anything else then, Jaan."

"Is that why we suffer, Tessa? So we may go

back to the garden appreciative?"

"Then do we harm ourselves, Jaan, by creating our own joy? Do we block our own return?"

"Maybe the Owl lied, Tessa."

"Then what was the point of all this, Jaan?"

He had no answer. The light beyond the archway was beautiful. But was it more beautiful than this bubble he created with Tessa? Was it more real?

***

Time was meaningless, but change did come. Jaan and Tessa ran aground at the site where a great battle had taken place. Guttering fires burned where once there were buildings, and the corpses of the Fell Hordes were strewn across the field, gutted and dismembered, weapons sticking out of their bestial bodies. The stench of carnage was overpowering. None lived. None to deliver torments. Jaan shivered as he scanned the sky where black clouds began to gather. He and Tessa had lost their balance. Cracks ran through their perfect, crystalline bubble. Shapes circled among the clouds, darker than black, misshapen windows into an abyss.

Tessa bent down among the corpses and lifted out a barbed whip. "Jaan," she said. "Take a weapon."

Jaan found a long knife and brandished it, looking up at the clouds. "Tessa, I don't think this will—" With the loud crack of rent air, the whip wrapped around his throat, and Tessa pulled. Jaan's eyes bulged. The barbs were cruel, but the agony of betrayal was pain beyond anything he'd experienced. That alone should have driven off the Birds.

"Quickly, Jaan! Hurt me!"

At last he understood. Jaan rammed the knife into Tessa's belly, haft deep, and twisted. She doubled over, but jerked the whip with her last strength, crushing his windpipe. The bubble shattered. In the garden of their mind they still held each other desperately, fighting for balance. *I'm sorry I'm sorry I'm sorry...*

Still the Birds circled.

They healed and struck. *Tessa*. Healed and struck. *Jaan*. Time was meaningless and the Birds circled, sometimes high, sometimes low. They rode raging rapids of pain and panic that crushed inwards on their ruined little garden. Its skies grew dark. Its trees blackened with rot. It was one thing to submit to torture, together. But to hurt each other... How much pain could he inflict on her, to save her? How long could he bear it? How long could she? The Birds were very low. Amidst the chaos, Jaan scrambled for a plan.

After gutting Tessa again, Jaan took her whip and bound her ravaged body, hand and foot. He stood over her, watching, drinking in the agony over what he must do to her, and hoping it would be enough, for both of them. The Birds circled. Tessa's bowels slithered back inside her body, and the skin slowly closed the wound. Her eyelids fluttered.

He stared down hard, scrutinizing her naked body with as much disgust as he could pour through his eyes. In their bubble-garden they learned to delight in each other's bodies, but back in Hell, the habits of shame were deep and strong. Betraying her this way would hurt her more than anything he could do with a knife. It would protect her.

"Jaan, don't..." Tessa tried to cover herself, but was unable to move. Her eyes widened in horror. Didn't she understand? No, she *mustn't* understand. If she understood, he would lose her.

"This, Tessa? This... *meat of yours*... is what kept me from entering the arch?" The Owl had hinted as much. His Maker would welcome only perfection.

"Jaan, please..."

"Your lies weren't enough for me, Tessa. You aren't enough. How much will I have to suffer to clean the filth you've put into me? How far have you pulled me away from my redemption?"

Tears streamed from Tessa's eyes. Jaan had considered everything he was telling her. But he had rejected it. Hadn't he? The effort to convince her to feel his betrayal required him almost to believe his words. He had to hate her just a little if he was to save her. The look on her face tore him apart. She was saving him too.

Then his lower lip trembled.

And she saw.

What remained of their connection was tiny and dark, a clouded crystal shard, but he felt a whisper through it. *Jaan?* It broke his resolve. *Tessa.*

Her tears ceased. Her expression softened. She understood. *I love you too*, she whispered through the bond.

The Birds swooped. Silently they wheeled and dove, and where they struck, holes of nothingness riddled her body.

"Tessa!" Jaan screamed.

They swarmed her, thick as flies on meat, and all Jaan could see was a flapping, churning void where Tessa lay bound. When they broke off, she was gone.

In every corner of his mind, Jaan was alone. He was aware of himself still screaming, wordlessly, until something inside him broke. The Birds swooped and circled. Jaan watched them impassively, suddenly as silent as they. "Come," he whispered. The Birds scattered in all directions, back to their clouds.

***

The man dragged his feet across the courtyard, towards the arch. Voices around him whispered. Eyes in pale faces watched, scrutinized his nakedness with revulsion. He ignored all of them. The Gatekeeper waited, black against the golden light spilling from within the arch. He shuffled towards him and stopped, his eyes downcast. He submitted to the groping claws on his body. He knew that yellow eyes examined every bit of his naked, emaciated flesh. It didn't matter. All his shame had burned away. His suffering was complete. He knew even before the Gatekeeper's bow that he could pass. He resumed his shuffle, into the blinding light.

The world beyond the arch was bathed in sunlight. The trees and sky were vivid shades of green and blue, and music and laughter were everywhere. Fountains splashed. A breeze carried the scents of flowers. Before him on the trim lawn was a long banquet table. Seated on both sides were huge birds of every sort, beaked and billed, crested and horned, chittering and honking merrily, their colored plumage ruffling in the breeze. In unison, their heads turned toward the man.

At the head of the table sat the Owl. He stood and bowed. His enormous eyes looked pleased. "At last," the Owl said. "You are ready." With a sweep of his wing, he gestured to a great, silver platter at the center of the table, garnished with a mixed assortment of human heads, limbs, and entrails. The man shuffled forward, noticing the cool softness of the grass under his feet, but caring nothing for it. He climbed onto the table and took his place, lying on his back. The sunlit sky filled his eyes, blue and perfect, and birdsong rang in his ears.

THE GALL
M. Regan

10.

She is woken by the scratching.

Skritch-skritch. Skritch-skritch. A nail grates against the grain, dead skin digging into dead wood. Dead wood moldering into rot. There is sickness in her belly as her thoughts decompose around the noise, the creep of it scurrying *up-down-up-down* the segmented tube of her spine.

She imagines millipedes. In her mind, they scurry out from beneath the closet door, small and thin and black. Like the jamb that they had penetrated: small and thin and black. Like herself: small. Thin. Black. She imagines their turgid bodies slipping into her ear, dry, bellies rasping against the canal; they spiral into the tight of her cochlea, thrashing and creaking with pleasure.

Her mind is full of legs. Tangled. Undulating. Scrape-scraping, trying to pry her open.

Skritch-skritch. Skritch-skritch.

There are some things that are not meant to be opened. Not now. Not yet.

She cocoons herself in last night's sweater, hiding her body in its knitted husk. Her eyes are closed, and she is counting.

Waiting.

9.

There is the idea of metamorphosis.

It is terrible, that idea. Horrifying. The thought of it haunts her as nightmares do, keeping her from sleep. How grotesque it is that caterpillars should become moths; and larva, lady beetles; and children, adults. How surreal it is to know that some nascent force will someday give a tug to the zipper of her DNA, and suddenly her body will be coming apart at the seams: stretching, warping, dissolving, melting down into the very basest of its components, returning to the primordial ooze from whence all life began. It is an inescapable change, a mutation that those affected await with an inbred sense of awareness. But after being reset within the mold of an imago, not even a butterfly will know its old self.

That is sad, she thinks.

Or maybe it is not sad.

She is in a liquid state. The wet of it rolls down her cheeks, murky with emotion and brackish with salt. Her insides threaten to sludge down her thighs.

In Hide-and-Seek, she suddenly remembers, it is the one who finds that has control. That then relinquishes control. From sought to seeker; the transformation is instantaneous and dramatic. It is powerful.

Change is happening.

Skritch-skritch. Skritch- skritch.

8.

When she was seven, she liked to hunt galls.

With the *crunch* of snow beneath her and a swath of pale clouds above, she would tromp the reed-lined paths of the marshlands, following the morass's outskirts and the fence that wended tipsily around the local electrical plant. It felt safer there, alone between rust and high voltage wires. During those frosty afternoons, she would play her own version of Hide-and-Seek, counting out the number of swollen stalks that lurked in plain sight.

She wondered if that was where the expression came from. To have gall. Daddy once told her that cheeky insects were to blame for the botanical phenomenon; they impregnated unlucky verdure with their eggs, then left them to grow bloated with parasites.

Her mother was due to have a baby soon. She did not know how to feel about that.

Bending low—mittens atop her knees, plumes streaming from her nostrils—she scrutinized the galls for signs of trauma. For forced penetration, or some hint of life.

Life finds a way, she had heard people say. Except for when it doesn't.

Coated like flesh upon skeletal boughs, the eleventh snowfall of winter gleamed. It was too white, she thought. A void that had swallowed the trees and the sky, that had blanketed all beneath its skin, and she might have quailed under the crushing, empty weight of oblivion had it not been for the plague-colored boils growing upon the greenery.

The world reflected in grays off of the sheen of her eyes, that lambent light draining through the entry-holes of her irises. Her lashes lowered.

If she listened closely, the girl believed she could hear it: the *skritch-skritch, skritch-skritch* of something inside, trying to be found.

Fighting to Become.

7.

"You promised me you'd give him a chance," Mother snaps. She is exasperated. A waspish anger buzzes against the backs of her teeth, its underlining drone having harmonized with the washing machine's motor.

The washing machine is always running, these days. The baby is one year old. Life is a mess. Within the unseen belly of the metal drum, liquids slosh and froth to foamy whiteness, the heave-hitch roiling of its insides rumbling through the linoleum.

Lain too-close, the floor tiles are starting to crack. The pulse of the load reverberates within her soles. It is nauseatingly rhythmic.

"You *promised* me, Nova."

She sits at the table, seeing tallies in the woodgrain. 1, 2, 3...

Skritch.

"Nova, are you even listening?!"

Her nail is dulled to bluntness. She could not leave a mark if she tried.

"Do you even *understand* what you're telling me?"

Her brother pounds his pudgy palms against the tray of his booster seat, his Very Hungry Caterpillar bib already caked in mashed potatoes. There is a membrane of gravy in his lap, gelatinous and cold; there is a smile upon his lips, and giggles wedged like mushed peas in the gap between his cheeks.

"*I* don't understand," Mother continues, tone fluxing between the quiet rage of a private rant and louder accusations. The kettle on the stove is growing louder, too. Shriller, screeching. A full-blown shriek rattles free of its throat, belched out along with a vaporous soul.

"*Christ*, Nova."

Curdled steam hovers just below the ceiling, staining the plaster with damp. It will rot, she thinks. Someday, everything will rot. But today, the palls of milky air simply disperse into the ether, evaporating without leaving any evidence behind. She wishes she could do the same.

"Why would you even say something like that? Why would you say something like that *now*?"

Mother listens to the screaming of the kettle. Mother listens to the screaming of the baby. She had wondered if Mother would listen to the screaming of her daughter.

"If this is some kind of tantrum, or a ploy for attention, you are too old for me to indulge it."

No.

"I'm not even going to acknowledge this anymore. Jesus."

So she, in turn, does not listen to Mother. The screaming of cicadas rings deafeningly within her ears, and she wishes that she were outside. In the yard. In the marsh.

In the closet.

Skritch.

6.

"First," she tells her brother, "we choose who will be It."

"What's It?" he asks, sprawled across the living room floor. The three-year-old's stubby legs peddle above him, and she is reminded of overturned beetles. It is not a kind thought. "Is It a boy or a girl?"

"It can be both," she explains. Her legs are crossed. But her fingers are drumming against her elbow, restless and skittering when she amends, "Or It could be neither, I guess. I don't know. It doesn't matter."

"But if It doesn' matter, then why're we choosin' an It?"

"Because It *does* matter. It is important. It starts the game. It finishes the game. Without an It, you can't do anything."

"I dun get it. I dun get It," her brother whines, rolling with a flail onto his stomach. Her eyes roll along with him. "I dun wanna play. I dun like this game."

"You will," she promises, snatching up the Wii controller that he had begun wriggling towards. She moves fast; his mood sours faster.

"No!"

With an audible *thud*, the boy's fist connects with the carpet. The seam of his lips is ripping wide—wider—too wide, and he gags up the yowl that had been lodged in the deep and the dark of his gullet. It breaks free of his body as a nymph erupts from its exoskeleton, and he is revolting to her.

"*No!* I dun like this game!"

She holds the desired remote high above her sibling's head, allowing it to dangle from its strap with the precariousness of a chrysalis. It spins; he wails. A snot bubble pops in one nostril. The bones of the child's ribcage strain against his overall bib, and his sister entertains the thought of the whole of him tearing in two. His stockinged heels beat against the ground, and she thinks that she hates him.

"*I dun wanna play!*" her brother mewls again. Spittle threatens to choke him with every new, wheezing keen. She half-wishes that it would. The other half of her doesn't know what to wish. Objections change pitch within her skull's inner chambers, his voice transmogrified by echoes and memories and insect husks. "*I dun wanna play! I dun wanna!*"

Protests surge up and up and over. They spill, slime drooling down his chin.

"*No!*"

Acid is threatening to spill down her own.

"*Nooooo!*"

She leaves, taking what little control she has with her.

5.

It is a calming technique, he tells her, counting backwards from ten.

10.

9.

8.

7.

He offers to help lead her, much as he offers to help with her buttons. They can even count on her buttons, if she likes. If she doesn't like.

6.

5.

4.

Count backwards from ten, he tells her.

3.

2.

1.

It will be over soon.

Ready or not, here I—

4.

Skritch-skritch, skritch-skritch.

"How many legs does a millipede have?"

She sits with her back to the closed closet door, her legs to her chest and her chin on her knees. She itches where there is contact. Where there had been contact does worse than itch.

"I know it's not one thousand. So why even call it a *milli*pede? You know?"

Planked oak resonates. Thrums. The reverberation of each scratch can be felt in ghostly aftershocks, scoring invisible lines into her spine. Vertebrae chatter on the braided chain of her nerve endings.

At least, she thinks the chattering is her vertebrae.

"It's just... It's stupid to call a thing something when it isn't that thing at all," she reasons with the noise. Her frown is deepening into a scowl, her attentions briefly snared by the glow-in-the-dark galaxies that Mother had plastered above her bed. The plastics' sallow gleam is an insult to the dead and the dying forces that had been strung in higher heavens.

"Am I the only one who sees that?"

Stars that are not stars, despite being called stars. A brother who is not a brother, even though he is her brother. A game that is not a game, given that she had not consented to play.

She swallows around a budding epiphany, the lump of it forming a gall in her throat.

"*Nova,*" Father calls from downstairs. "*Come out, come out. It's dinnertime.*"

Skritch-skritch.

3.

She promised.

Skritch-skritch.

That much is true, at least. She did promise. She did say that she would give him a chance.

Skritch-skritch, skritch-skritch.

But what exactly does it mean to give someone a chance? Parasites might deserve a chance, but so do the stalks left engorged in their wake, stuffed too-full and suffering for it. Her game of Hide-and-Seek had deserved a chance, though her brother had been too young, too spoiled, to understand as much. Certainly she deserves a chance, as well: a chance to run, if nothing else.

She deserves a fair chance.

But life is unfair. Adults are unfair. And so she is compelled to conduct herself by double standards and inconsistent, broken rules as he finds her and finds her and finds her.

He counts backwards from ten, but by then it is too late to hide.

He counts backwards from ten, leaving slugs across her hip.

He counts backwards from ten, and she decides to give him the same number of chances.

She will keep her promise to Mother, even if he won't.

2.

"What's It?"

"It can be anyone. A boy, a girl. It doesn't matter. It's not important. What *is* important is It. It is important. It is the most important."

"What does It do?"

"It waits."

"That's all?"

"No. It is the start and the finish, you see. It closes its eyes in the dark, and It counts backwards from ten. It keeps a tally. From ten to one to zero. And while It counts, you run and you hide so you're never-ever-ever found."

"I don't wanna be found?"

"Definitely not."

"Why not?"

"Because It hasn't always been It. It used to be someone else. But after you're found, things change. You change. You become It. Then you *are* It."

"I don't wanna change!"

"You have to. Everyone changes."

"Well, what if I don't play?"

"You have to play. Everyone plays."

"Why?"

"Because I want everyone to play. If they don't, the game won't be any fun at all."

"This is a game?"

"No."

"You're scaring me, Nova..."

"Then maybe you should hide."

1.
Change is happening.
10.
It begins in her fingertips. In her toes. It forms a little grub within her tissues, a maggot that even now is eating away at flesh that should have died. That did not die.
9.
Life finds a way, they say. Even when it is not wanted. It hides in wait. It waits.
8.
She is a reedy thing now, but gall has seen to it that she won't stay that way much longer. The space beneath her belly has given its first ligneous groan of distension. Of metamorphosis. The husk of Who She Was is crackling into fragments, for she is now too large to fit inside her childhood skin. It cannot contain her anymore. She is growing, evolving, *becoming* what she always was, what she was always going to be, and it should frighten her.
7.
It does not frighten her.
6.
Calmly, methodically, she is counting down the buttons on her blouse.
5.
Her shirt crumples with the chittering of chitin, molting from her shoulders in a crust of gossamer. It keeps her old-shape as it falls, though she has forgotten it even before it hits the carpet. A shell, sloughed. Superfluous. *Skritch-skritch, skritch-skritch.*
4.
Butterflies have begun to tremble beneath her wrists, exposed and clinging upside-down to violet veins. They quiver, anticipatory, while they wait for the drying of their wings. In a few moments, they will be flying. In a few moments more, they will not remember a life before flying. They are changed now. Free now. Hideous now, their painted eyes windows to

soullessness.

3.

They are beautiful. Caterpillars become moths, larvae become lady beetles, children become adults; it is a grotesque process, but oh-so-very fascinating. An inescapable mutation, and there is simply no way to stop it once it has begun.

2.

It has begun.

1.

Skritch-skritch, skritch-skritch, skritch-skritch.

0.

She opens the closet door.

"I found you."

O.

"What do you want to be when you grow up?" Mother had asked, her attentions on her six-year-old and her clippers around a rose. Its *snip* cuts short an idle song. It had also cleaved a blossom's neck, one head falling to the left while the other tumbled to the right. The sweet scent of sward and heat and summer rain teased at the girl's nose, mimicking the tickle of the caterpillar inching over its bridge.

"I wanna be a person with lots of friends," the girl had chirped in answer, grinning bright. The tips of her smile met the ends of the caterpillar, the arc and the arch conjoining to form a ring-around-the-rosie. Or a scream. She added, "I wanna have a party an' play Hide-and-Seek with everyone. That's the best game."

"Oh?" Mother chuckled, her amusement underscored by a silvery sweep of her shears. "That sounds great. And I bet you'll make lots of friends in your new school. But... When you have that party, love, I hope you only invite those friends that I can see."

The words had not fully left her before they were rebuffed. Her daughter shook her head, pigtails tangling in the grass.

"No. Everyone. It's only fun if we all play together."

"But don't you think it would be nicer if only *real—*"

"You said Daddy is real. He's real, even though we can't see him anymore. You said he's here, watchin' over us. That he's here for me. *You* said."

"Well, yes. Yes, but I think that your new friends would like you *better* if—"

"*No*, Mama. Listen. *Everyone*."

Though she could not see it, the child had known her Mother was rolling her eyes. She could hear it, just as clearly as she could hear the snapping of a branch. The twig had broken with a sound like a finger. Mother sighed, and another pruned gall rolled away.

It was too bad, the girl had thought, that

125

Mother had to kill the roses for sins committed by pests. But once corrupted, there was nothing else that could be done. Once found, they could not be tolerated. They had to die, and that was that. All of them. Too bad, so sad.

Snip.

As the caterpillar slid down the curve of her cheek, the six-year-old had reached out for one of those decapitated galls, holding it to her ear in parody of a beach shell. It was a trick that Daddy had taught her. She missed Daddy. She listened like he had told her to.

"Right, well. Do me a favor, Nova, and hide that 'special friend' of yours away when Gale is here, okay? Give Gale a chance before scaring him with... Just give him a chance."

It was not the sound of the sea that she heard.

"*Okay*, Nova?"

What she heard was silence.

"Okay."

GATEKEEPER
Andrea L. Staum

Gatekeeper, Gatekeeper open for me!
The city is burning and no one can leave.
My armies are amassing outside the gate
and there is no path outside the wall to take.
My men will end this torture quick.
Your people are crying for reprieve from flame.
Allow us entry and you will receive my mercy
as it falls upon all those who assist.

Gatekeeper, Gatekeeper, do as you are told and open
       the gate!
Death does not care which way it takes them.
Would you see your people burn rather than flee or
let them fall to the water and attempt to swim away?
Many have taken flight from the walls to escape.
Flames do not discriminate as they make way.
Allow your people to choose their own fate.
Can you not hear them crying for mercy?

Gatekeeper, Gatekeeper, you have your duty and I
       have mine,
Safe passage and mercy cannot help the damned.
Your will is strong which I admire.
Such loyalty will be rewarded—I will give you freedom.
With your last breath you would keep me at bay?
Think I will allow you to continue your obstinate
       bloodline?
Now allow my armies to take your streets.
Death by sword is quicker than incineration.

Gatekeeper, Gatekeeper, your will is strong,
but I have already won.
Do you not see your mayor has surrendered
and there is nothing more for you to do?
Stand aside and let my army through.
Surely you see that although flame may be quenched
bloodlust cannot, as war cries become battle song.
You are already condemning them all!

Gatekeeper, Gatekeeper accept your destiny and quell
 your fears!
The flames have come to lick your back and you know
 it is done.
I am a demon of my word and one more twist of my
 wrist will set you free,
I never said how your freedom would come.
Your God has forsaken you in your time of need.
You have done well unwavering in your duty, but,
the end was written in the pages of time long before
 your years.
Onward, men, we take the city tonight and end
 this siege.

THE GARDEN OF METAMORPHOSIS
Terje Nordin

You come to, a little disoriented. Unsure of where you are and what you were doing, you look around. You seem to be standing in your apartment. The ambient light from the windows tells you it's in the middle of the day. You would normally be at work at this time, but you are not, so you were certainly doing something more important...

A harsh, bitter smell interrupts your thoughts. Like blood and sweat.

Looking around for the source of the stench, you can't help but linger at your television set—it is a bit rounded, bulging strangely, almost sagging in places. You step closer to investigate. You reach out. Its surface is covered in fine light hairs and feels warm to your skin.

A noise behind you catches your attention, as if a chorus of frogs were attempting to sing the song of birds. You turn your head to the window and see that the world outside does not resemble the world you remember. There is no street; there are no apartment blocks, no shops, no cars. As far as you can see, there is only a smooth plain splotched in shades of beige and pink and covered in what looks like sparse hair.

There are soft squelching sounds as you turn between the grotesque fleshscape and the bizarrely organic TV. The floor is soft and warm and throbs slowly as if with a beating heart. You get on your hands and knees to get a closer look, and the surface yields more than it should. From your position, you can see behind the sofa, and notice a small pink growth sprouting from the wall there.

Investigate the TV — page 131.
Investigate the sprout on the wall — page 132.
Go outside — page 134.

With so many strange transformations surrounding you, the matter of the television appears to be the easiest one to approach. Pushing the knob of cartilage found where the switch used to be makes the TV hum and sends a ripple racing across the skin that has become its screen. The elastic surface stretches outward into violent shapes that arrange themselves into what vaguely approximate a nose and mouth. The jaw opens, hissing static and a weak light from the cavity. Further down the throat is the source of the light. You lean in for a closer look and the jaws clench down around your upper half. The giant lips pin your arms to your sides, and you can feel the tongue against your belly. A claustrophic pressure builds around you as the gullet undulates in a swallowing motion. The walls of the shaft are lubricated with a moist mucus that makes your descent swift. All the while, static emits from the radiance you are plummeting toward.

You land with a splash in a viscous fluid which smells like sour milk. The roaring static is deafening, and the flickering light temporarily blinds you. Hanging above you is a swollen sack of skin, from which the sound and light are emanating.

To your left is a small, round opening in the wall. It is the only visible exit from this moist stomach chamber.

Touch the skin sack — page 135.
Push through the wall orifice — page 136.

The pink-colored protuberance on the wall resembles an oversize nipple. As you trace your finger along the areola, the wrinkled mound of skin at its center stiffens. A little moisture leaks from within. Gaping wide, you ease the nipple between your lips and suck like an infant. A warm and thick effluvium streams into your mouth. It is sweet, with a heat that touches the back of your throat and warms the belly. After swallowing your fill, you lean against the wall, soft like the floor beneath you. You listen to the pulse of strange vessels in the wall, full and content.

The walls seem to grow close. The air is clammy and your limbs have started to itch. Unable to stand the thick air and tightening walls, you heave to your feet and push through the door, tight in its opening.

The stairs to the ground floor resemble bone and cartilage. The descent takes much longer than you would expect. You step out of the organic stairwell onto the plain of skin that stretches as far as you can see.

You grow weary travelling from the complex and begin to sweat. The itch in your limbs has become a dull ache creeping into your bones. Vertigo drives you to your knees next to a large strand of hair. Your limbs twitch with spasms and the once pleasant heat in your stomach grows fiery. The taste of blood and bile fills your mouth. Thick cords erupt from your legs and bury themselves in the ground. You can feel your spine twisting and cracking, splitting, stretching into a branching trunk over four meters tall. Almost expected now, what were once your arms grow long, your fingers spouting bone-colored twigs.

You dominate this landscape, dwarfing the hair strand that, moments before, dwarfed you. Your instincts run rampant, a cycle of desires: to spread your seed, or to rest.

Grow fruit — page 137.
Don't grow fruit — page 138.

The stairwell is dim and murky, with a humid, unnatural breeze. The descent is uneventful, save for the fact the stairs now closely resemble a skeleton supporting the flesh-like walls. What would be the front door of the apartment complex is missing, replaced by a tall hole in the wall. It reminds you of a hatchet wound in a young tree.

Outside, your suspicions seem to be confirmed: the plains stretch endlessly in all directions. The texture of the ground is that of leathered skin, firmer than the floor of your apartment. You wonder if digging into it would yield a layer of fat tissue. A gentle wind caresses you. The few strands of hair you see sway like slim, branchless trees. The sun has passed its zenith across the sky, continuing westward.

You trek across the plains of flesh. A shape other than a hair strand emerges in the distance. Six legs carry a carapace the color of ripe cherries over the bruised land.

Avoid the creature — page 139.
Approach the creature —page 140.

Standing on your toes, you can barely graze the flashing, tumorous growth. The soft skin reacts to your touch by going loose and flowing down your arms like molten wax. It has a firm hold on you, enveloping you, dragging you upward in a similar swallowing motion as the television used to bring you to this chamber. A wave of exhaustion rushes through your being. The bright lights dim; the static softens to a murmur.

There is comfort here. You sleep.

When you awaken, an indeterminate time has passed. Your skin is stiff and dry. Moving your limbs feels difficult: too many legs, or possibly too many arms. Six insect limbs shed from your skin and pull you up from the soft ground. The remains of your cocoon hangs from your newly hardened carapace, and you shake it to the ground.

The dark cavity you are in has a single exit. You stumble into the canal, growing stronger and more sure with each step. As you become accustomed to your new locomotion, your antennae warn you of a bifurcation in the tube-like passage.

Go left — page 146.
Go right — page 147.

The orifice leads to a dark, winding tunnel coated in a warm slime. You arrive at a crossroads: the left passage appears to dive deeper into the fleshy fortress, while the right slants upwards.

Go left — page 146.
Go right — page 148.

You lost your eyes in the transformation, but the vibrations in the ground are enough of a warning: something is approaching. A mass moves closer and halts. It plucks your single fruit from your branch and continues its trek past you.

There are no other visitors. Your senses grow duller. You can feel your trunk shriveling into a husk. Time becomes immaterial.

Darkness envelops you — page 129.

You fight the urge to grow fruit, and, in doing so, incite a new series of changes within your anatomy. Your interior is slowly remolding about itself. New appendages, new organs. You tremble and shake. Your outer layers have become dead and stiff, and they shed from your new frame with each spasm. You spread your new wings, paper thin, allowing them to dry in the sun.

You take flight and soar free over the plain of flesh. Some details immediately garner your attention. There is a large creature with a thick red shell traversing the plains on six thin limbs. Beyond it, there is a large depression in the landscape, vaguely circular, with a wrinkled knob of flesh at its center. Westward of both is a globular body precariously balanced on a slim stem.

Investigate the carapaced creature — page 140.
Land in the circular depression — page 143.
Inspect the globular mass — page 144.

You come upon a curious tree growing from the fleshy ground. The branches reach like contorted arms, and there is a pattern on the trunk that uncannily resemble a human face. A single fruit hangs from a branch, fat, violet, and bulbous with juice.

Eat the fruit — page 145.
Continue across the plain — page 142.

The large arthropod takes notice of you. The two of your begin to converge on a shared path. Its compound eyes seem to look past you, or through you, and its mandibles are clicking with excitement. The monstrosity is swift, and pins you to the soft earth with a single front leg. It bends over and rips a large strip of flesh from your abdomen. You are aware of your viscera gushing from your torso, staining the fleshy ground below you a dark crimson.

Darkness envelops you — page 129.

The two-legged creature seems eager to get close to you and veers in your direction. You can smell its soft body, something alien in this alien world. Your mandibles clatter and your instincts scream through your mind. Before you are aware of your actions, you've speared the biped to the ground and are ripping its flesh from its bones. Its flesh is warm and exhilarating.

Your appetite satisfied, you once again contemplate the tree on the horizon. Its surreal angles are both enticing and terrifying to your insectoid mind.

Approach the tree — page 139.
Avoid the tree — page 142.

In due time you reach a large, circular valley embossed in the meatscape. At its centre is a trembling mound of wrinked flesh, different from the surrounding flesh. Beyond the valley is another fleshy mass, rounder, perched atop a stem.

Enter the valley — page 143.
Circumvent the valley towards the stem — page 144.

Almost immediately after setting foot in the valley area, the wrinkled mass of flesh opens to reveal a pharynx lined with dastardly rows of curved teeth. A long tentacular tongue rockets outward and wraps around your legs. With alarming rapidity you are dragged toward the saliva-rimmed maw. You fall.

Darkness envelops you — page 129.

A long stem propels the globe towards the sky. Like all things here, the body appears to have an organic skin. There is a band of hair growing around the equator of the globe.

As you get near, the skin pulls away towards the poles, revealing a white hemisphere surrounding a dark hole. The stalk bends, and the eye focuses on you. The pupil is a well that you could drown in. You see yourself reflected on the eye's glassy surface.

Vertigo.

Are you staring at the eye? Or are you staring at this speck of flesh with your great cyclopic vision? Does it make a difference?

Darkness envelops you — page 129.

As expected, the fruit is soft and juicy in your mouth. Every bite is an explosion of sensations impossible to categorize. There are nuances of lilac and violet. Your inner ear picks up the rich sweetness of the pulp. The soles of your feet feel the piquant aftertaste. Liquid fire flows through your mortal body and sets your mind aflame. You fall back, content. You are one with all, and all within one.

Darkness envelops you – page 129.

You lose your footing as the slope falls steeply. The space grows narrow, and you fall until the fleshy walls hugs you close.

A second or an eon passes. Your body dissolves and reintegrates with your prison of meat. Your eyes atrophy. The tubing of your body, your intestines and veins and others besides, joins the complex series of passages you were once lost in. Your teeth grow numerous and sharp. What was once you is kneaded and stretched, pushing what remains of your head through the surface of the planet. You feel the sun on your wrinkled scalp. Your mind collapses on itself, replaced only with an infernal infinite hunger.

Darkness envelops you — page 129.

The tunnel leads to a sphincter that draws away from your quivering antennae. Fresh air billows into the passage, replacing the putrid stink you were just wallowing in. Beyond the portal are the plains of skin, pink and beige in their glory.

A gnarled tree is visible on the horizon. Approaching from the east is a strange creature with two legs.

Approach the tree — page 139.
Approach the two-legged creature — page 141.
Avoid both — page 149.

The tunnel ends in a sphincter that pushes you through in a sensation of birth. You are covered in slime, dripping onto the meatscape. Jutting from the endless expanse is a branching growth, somehow fruiting in this hell.

Approach the tree — page 139.
Go east – page 142.
Go west — page 149.

You find a spot where nothing obscures the horizon in all directions. You sit down, facing the setting sun, and turn your attention inwards. You close your eyes. Your breathing becomes longer, slower, deeper. You become aware of your thoughts as wisps of cloud passing over an empty sky. Your mentality devolves further, becoming nothing more than a mind's eye observing the vast emptiness within yourself.

Time becomes nebulous. How long have you been here? Have you always been here?

Something disturbed your inner harmony. You rush back to your physical being and direct your attention to the thing that now approaches. Is it something same, or something new? Is it something other, or something you? Does it make a difference?

Darkness envelops you — page 129.

ABOUT THE AUTHORS

Kyle E. Miller is the author of short stories, poems, and essays appearing in such places as *Betwixt Magazine*, *Lackington's*, and *Thoreau On Mackinac*. He currently resides in Michigan, his lifelong home and the birthplace of his imagination. He is probably wandering around somewhere trying not to catch the fish of his thoughts. One day, he'd like to become a hermit.

Ian Ableson is an ecologist by training and a writer by choice; he has experience as a naturalist, a planetarium operator, a nocturnal-animal-educational-program-presenter, and a museum tour guide who actually got paid to talk to children about dinosaurs. Although this is his first time being published as an author of fiction, his name is attached to two ecological papers about the surprisingly fascinating relationships between ants and aphids (which he highly encourages you to research if you're not familiar with them).

LaVa Payne lives in the Piney Woods of east Texas where she writes stories and explores old sawmill towns.

Virginia Chase Sutton's chapbook, *Down River*, has recently been released. Her second book, *What Brings You to Del Amo*, won the Samuel French Morse Poetry Prize, and is being reissued this year by Doubleback Books. *Embellishments* is her first book and *Of a*

Transient Nature is her third. Sutton's poems have won a poetry scholarship to Bread Loaf Writer's Conference, the Allen Ginsberg Poetry Award, and the National Poet Hunt. Seven times nominated for the Pushcart Prize, her poems have appealed in *The Paris Review*, *Ploughshares*, *Peacock Journal*, *Comstock Review*, and many other literary publications, journals, and anthologies. She lives in Tempe, Arizona.

Tiffany Morris is a writer from Nova Scotia. Her horror fiction and poetry have appeared in *Eye to the Telescope*, *Augur*, *Room Magazine*, and anthologies from Clash Books and Carrion Blue 555, among others. Find her online at tiffmorris.com or Twitter @tiffmorris.

Frederick L. Shiels is a poet and (still teaching) Prof. Emeritus of Politics and History at Mercy College, NY. He has been published in *Avocet*, *Deep South Review*, *The Hudson River Anthology*, *The New Verse News*, and his most recent book is *Preventable Disasters: Why Governments Fail*.

Dr. Jackie Ferris is a writer who likes pushing cutting edge boundaries. She has worked in the mental health field in several European countries and has appeared in several mental health journals, magazines, and videos.

Sara Tantlinger resides outside of Pittsburgh on a hill in the woods. She is the author of the dark poetry collections *The Devil's Dreamland* and *Love For Slaughter*, along with several other poems, flash fictions, and a few short stories. She is a poetry editor for The Oddville Press, a member of the SFPA, and an active HWA member. She can be found lurking in graveyards or on Twitter @SaraJane524.

R. Bremner of northeast New Jersey, USA, writes of incense, peppermints, and the color of time in such venues as *International Poetry Review*, *Anthem: A Leonard Cohen Tribute Anthology*, and *Climate of Change: Sigmund Freud In Poetry*. He has twice won Honorable Mention in the Allen Ginsberg awards (2016, 2017). You'll find his thirteen eBooks at Amazon, Lulu, B&N, and other eBook retailers. Ron invites you to visit his Instagram poetry at beat_poet1 and absurdist_poet.

Joanna Koch's short fiction has been published in journals such as *Dark Fuse* and *Hello Horror*, and included in several speculative and dark fiction anthologies. Joanna is an MA Contemplative Psychotherapy graduate of Naropa University who currently lives and works near Detroit. Follow her monstrous musings at horrorsong.blog.

Rajiv Moté is a writer living in Chicago whose stories have appeared in *Unlikely Story* and *Cast of Wonders*. He spent so long staring at *The Garden of Earthly Delights* for his piece that the figures haunt his peripheral vision. He purges excess words on Twitter @RajivMote.

M. Regan has been writing in various capacities for over a decade, with credits ranging from localization work to scholarly reviews, advice columns to short stories. Particularly fascinated by those fears and maladies personified by monsters, she enjoys composing dark fiction, studying supernatural creatures, and traveling to places with rich histories of folklore.

Andrea L. Staum is the author of the *Dragonchild Lore* series, *The Attic's Secret* novella, *Scattered Dreams* short story collection, and has contributed to several bestselling anthologies. She's a trained motorcycle technician, an amateur home renovator, and somehow manages to find time to write. She lives in south central Wisconsin with her husband and three overlords... err... cats.

Terje Nordin lives in Umeå, Sweden and works as a librarian. He writes role-playing games and records noise music.

CATALOGUE BLUE 555

CB555-01: 555 Vol. 1: None So Worthy
CB555-02: The Book of Adventures
CB555-03: Mr. Malin and the Night
CB555-04: Haiku Fuck You
CB555-05: 555 Vol. 2: This Head, These Limbs
CB555-06: The Book of Adventures 2
CB555-07: A Terrible Thing
CB555-08: 555 Vol. 3: Questions & Cancers
CB555-09: Savage Anesthesia
CB555-10: Honey & Sulphur

Lightning Source UK Ltd.
Milton Keynes UK
UKHW040807210819
348311UK00001B/34/P